"FUNNY AND INVENTIVE."

—*Booklist*

"In this smart, fast-paced metaphysical thriller, Jenny McPhee brings the insights of quantum mechanics to bear upon love, stardom, and the baffling uncertainties of human behavior. *The Center of Things* is a brilliant debut by a writer of exceptional talent and promise."

—AMITAV GHOSH

Author of *The Glass Palace*

"This dense, witty debut novel, a kind of mystery, steers its self-doubting heroine between the demands of lust and intellectual fulfillment."

—*Daily News*

"With Marie, McPhee has created a warm and likable character, a protagonist whose flaws we grow protective of, a woman whose many mysteries intrigue."

—*Book* magazine

Please turn the page for more reviews....

the center
of things

JENNY McPHEE

Ballantine Books · New York

for luca

the center of things

1

{ T I M E }

"Most of life is wasted time."
—JOHN BERRYMAN

"I read poetry to save time."
—MARILYN MONROE

*"The distinction between past, present and future is
only an illusion, even if a stubborn one."*
—ALBERT EINSTEIN

Marie was early. And when Marie was early, she agonized.
During the first five minutes, she simply couldn't believe the
fact that she was early yet again. Then she began hating herself. It started with hating herself for being early, but she soon
moved on to hating herself for having dropped out of graduate
school, for not being married, for being partially deaf in one
ear, for writing for a tabloid, for being already thirty-nine years

old, for having straight hair, for not having children, for never finishing the philosophy of science paper she had been working on for nearly fifteen years, for being five feet eleven and three-quarters inches tall. When Marie could no longer bear her checklist of miseries, she started calculating the number of hours, to date, she had wasted by being early, and, based on those numbers and her life expectancy, how many more she would waste in the future.

According to Marco, hers was an uncommon case of reaction formation to the very common fear of abandonment. He had explained to her that most people react to the fear of abandonment associated with time appointments by being late themselves. Or they counter the fear by being compulsively on time. "But you, Marie," he had said, "anticipate the fear, as if by creating the same conditions earlier in time you can cancel out what you expect to occur later on. It is beautifully symmetrical, perfectly logical."

It seemed grossly illogical to Marie, who continued to add up the hours of her wasted life on a bar napkin at the Ear Inn. She worked as a researcher and reporter for the *Gotham City Star*, Manhattan's only remaining evening tabloid, and one of her duties for the paper was to gather material for the advancer file, which contained the obituaries of people not yet dead. She had come to the bar in a similar capacity—but this time she would also be writing the story herself. Marco called her obituary work a kind of literary pre-necrophilia and a prime example of her neurotic need to anticipate abandonment.

Just the day before, Nora Mars, the 1960s glamour queen

and actress, had suffered a massive cerebral hemorrhage and was in a coma. Despite her relative youth—she was sixty-two—and her otherwise excellent health, she was by all medical accounts unlikely to recover. News of the tragedy had devastated Marie. Since Marie was about ten years old, Nora Mars had been her most revered idol.

Nora Mars was the girl next door gone awry, in both looks and attitude—she had white-blond hair and a peaches-and-cream complexion, but her slanted green eyes made her look like some exotic hybrid. ("My mother passed over the postman for the Chinese laundryman," she had once notoriously told the press.) Her atypical beauty and hard-edged innocence combined to form Marie's teenage idea of female perfection.

Growing up, Marie had fantasized about being any number of movie stars she had come to know by watching endless hours of late night television. Before her parents were divorced, when she was eight, television had been allowed for only one hour on Saturday mornings. But after her father left, her mother stopped caring so much about rules, and Marie, over the following years, more than made up for her early childhood deprivation. The television set was on from the time she got home from school until she left again the next morning. She was a devotee of *The 4 O'Clock Movie*, *The Million Dollar Movie*, *Movie Playhouse*, *Late Nite at the Movies*, and *The Late Late Late Movie*. By high school she had few friends and rarely went out except to the movies, accompanied by her younger brother, Michael.

With Michael as her interlocutor, she honed her tastes. She

thought Katharine Hepburn overzealous and Doris Day whined too much; she preferred Gene Kelly to Fred Astaire but couldn't resist *Easter Parade*. She swooned over the soft-spoken Gary Cooper, adored the bumbling Jimmy Stewart, and wanted to marry the boisterous and charming Cary Grant.

In the end, however, the movies Marie came to love above all others were the noirs starring small shifty men—the kind you shouldn't marry—like Humphrey Bogart, George Raft, Peter Lorre, Alan Ladd, and James Cagney. As for the women, she worshipped the femmes fatales played by actresses such as Hedy Lamarr, Joan Crawford, Bette Davis, Lauren Bacall, Barbara Stanwyck, Rita Hayworth, Ava Gardner, Gloria Grahame, Gene Tierney, and Veronica Lake. But if she could have chosen to look and act like anyone in the world, it would have been Nora Mars.

Nora Mars did bad things and bad things happened to her both in real life and in her movies, and even so she always came out ahead. Sometimes, with all her husbands and scandals, she seemed to be on a mission to outrage and shock the public. But then she would make some comment or say some line, and the tangled truth of it would be so surprising that Marie, along with most of the country, just loved her even more. Nora Mars, Marie concluded, was a complete contradiction. While she needed to be loved by everybody, she did everything she could to make them hate her. She was a conformist who refused to conform, and her deep vulnerability was her greatest strength.

Over time, Marie and Michael began to write down and

then memorize lines of movie dialogue they particularly liked, and during the two years they overlapped in high school, whenever they crossed paths in the halls, they would quote one-liners at each other and see who could name the title, actor, and date of the movie first.

("For all I know, eternity could be time on an ego trip." Nora Mars, *The Reckoning*, 1959.)

Marie still played the game with herself sometimes, but it inevitably made her think of Michael, who had moved to L.A. fifteen years earlier and hadn't spoken to her since. He was the only person on earth who would be able to hear that Nora Mars line and understand precisely how Marie was feeling in that moment, as she sat in a bar obsessing about time wasted, time lost, time yet to be spent, as she waited to interview Nora Mars' third husband out of five—Rex Mars. (A renowned stipulation in Nora Mars' standard prenuptial agreement was that her husbands had to take her name and keep it even in the eventuality of divorce.) On Marie's napkin, the figures showed that so far she had wasted 10,264 hours of her life waiting.

Marie avoided dwelling on the past and rarely mentioned her brother to anyone, just as she scrupulously had told absolutely no one at the *Star*, not Brewster, not even Ned, about her passion for science and in particular for quantum mechanics. For some reason, however, she had found herself telling Marco about both. She had met him over a year ago in the Richard B. Salomon Reading Room of the New York Public Library's Science, Industry and Business Library, in the former

B. Altman department store building. She went there whenever she got the chance to work on her philosophy of science
paper, begun fifteen years ago during the second semester of
her first and only year of graduate school in philosophy. The
paper was for a seminar on the relationship between quantum
mechanics and reality. Learning about quantum theory—the
theory that describes the strange microscopic properties of elementary matter—had introduced Marie to a whole new way
of perceiving the world. Quantum theory showed that a particle can have potential existences in many places at once until
we look at it—only when it is measured by an observer does it
become "real" or fixed in one reality. For the minuscule stuff
that makes up all matter, reality depends upon who is looking.
The idea was at once disturbing and exciting to Marie, and she
had become obsessed with trying to grasp what was essentially
ungraspable.

("Be everywhere, do everything, and never fail to astonish."
Nora Mars, *Lightning*, 1972.)

And Marie was convinced that if she could just finish the
paper, return to graduate school, and get her Ph.D., she would
find an intellectually stimulating job in a small liberal arts
college, write meaningful articles for prestigious philosophy
journals, fall in love with a colleague, get married, have two
children, buy a house and a Volvo, and pursue a beautiful future.

This conviction drove her to the public library—first to the
Forty-second Street branch, now to the Thirty-fourth Street

branch, which was conveniently located three blocks south of the *Star*—year in and year out, filling up every free moment she had. For fifteen years the philosophy of science paper had been her greatest immediate goal in life. Every other activity of hers, which amounted to her job and her trips to revival movie theaters, was secondary, the time spent engaged in them stolen from what was of true and utmost importance to her. Her paper and all it symbolized represented the expression of her true self.

Marie and Marco first met during a snowstorm. She remembered because the library had stayed open late even though the entire city had been gradually shutting down due to the heavy snowfall. Earlier that day from her desk at the *Star*, Marie had watched as the Empire State Building, looming right outside the window, disappeared into a thick gray haze. As the afternoon progressed, the mood at the paper became a sort of frenzied glee. The Weather Channel was playing on the television in the conference room, and a constant swarm of people hovered around it. By three o'clock most of the staff had left, the writers filing three hours before deadline so that they could go home. Marie did the same, polishing a couple of runner dumps she had taken that morning. (Runners were reporters that called in and verbally dumped their stories on people like Marie who would then write them up.) The first was on an early morning brawl involving five men wearing tuxedos on the front steps of the Plaza Hotel after a charity ball. The fight was allegedly over an unidentified woman. The second was about a Staten Island resident who threw a cat off the ferry on his way to work on Wall Street. The cat's owner, a woman, was identified as the man's next-door neighbor. Neither was available for comment, but according to another neighbor, the cat's killer and the cat's owner were having an affair.

Marie was drawn to tabloid journalism because of stories like these. She was intrigued by how the stories were the same old ones yet managed to fascinate every time due to a slight altering of the details. It was a paradox: the convoluted, twisted, preposterous things people did every day were somehow never perceived as usual. And daily, she was witness to the fact that if you talked to anyone long enough, that person had a story to tell, a skeleton in the closet, or a secret tragedy. But the aspect of her job that challenged Marie the most was trying to understand people's motivations for what they did. It was a rigorous task, one that required an ability to tolerate high levels of ambiguity, because just when you thought you'd figured someone out, you'd see another possibility for what was driving that person. Of course, the subtleties of character motivation rarely, if ever, made it onto the page of a tabloid, but that was simply one more occupational hazard.

Oddly, the greatest obstacle to Marie's career moving forward was probably the fact that she loved to write. Because of it, she had gotten into the bad habit of ghosting for her peers at the *Star*. Both runners *and* writers came to her with the bare bones of a story, pleading, begging, even crying for her to help them out. So many of them anguished over the writing, while to Marie it came easily. She liked taking a few facts, a few quotes, a little filler, and scrambling them around until they fit together into some sort of recognizable whole. "Sure," she would say, "no sweat."

It all began with Ned Brilliant, who was a senior staff writer, although three years younger than she, when she first joined the *Star*. Marie had started late in journalism and figured ghosting for her peers might make up for the career years she had lost to her graduate school fiasco followed by five years of waiting tables while she "figured things out." When she got the job at the *Star*, she had the bright idea that she would prove to her colleagues how quickly she learned by doing their work, and they, in turn, would welcome her into their ranks. But it hadn't quite worked out that way. Ned had made it up to her by having an affair with her for several years and then jilting her when he got a better job at the *Post*.

But even that infamy hadn't put an end to her routinely composing other people's stories for no credit. The truth was that for Marie, writing *Star* pieces was like doing a jigsaw puzzle or building a model airplane—after she was finished she was left with a deeply satisfying sense of having made something, finished something. And it took so little effort—but that was also the problem. Marie never felt like her newspaper writing was any sort of real accomplishment, so why take any credit for it? In churning out stories for the *Star*, she experienced none of the torture, the insanity, or the gut-wrenching that accompanied the writing of her philosophy of science paper. And that was a very real, and ongoing, failure.

The Science, Industry and Business Library was usually

packed with a wide range of pleasantly anonymous humanity—mostly male—but on the day of the snowstorm the building was virtually empty when Marie arrived just after five o'clock. She paused for a second in the ellipse-shaped lobby to let the snow melt off her. Chiseled into the gently curving wall were quotations from the luminaries of science, industry, and business. She read, "Next to knowing all about your own business, the best thing to know is all about the other fellow's business.—John D. Rockefeller." That quote, she thought, should be on the *Gotham City Star*'s masthead.

Marie went to the Salomon Reading Room and was disappointed to find someone sitting in her favorite cubicle next to the microform and patents room. She decided instead to sit in one of the faux-leather armchairs and reread Abner Shimony's article on "Metaphysical Problems in the Foundations of Quantum Mechanics." A small man was sitting in the chair next to hers reading the *American Journal of Forensic Medicine and Pathology*. An unkempt stack of newspapers and magazines was on the floor next to him. Marie glanced at him quickly before she sat down: square face, sleek raven hair with a slight wave and parted on the side, olive skin, dark wide-set eyes, a full-lipped mouth, a thin mustache, and a goatee. He wore a loose-fitting navy-blue suit that could have been pajamas or a Chinese Communist Party uniform.

After about twenty minutes, when the man had worked his way through half his pile of magazines and newspapers, which ranged from the *Weekly Compilation of Presidential Docu-*

ments to the *National Enquirer,* he turned to Marie and said, "I noticed you were reading about physics and I was wondering if I might ask you a related question."

"Sure," Marie said, thinking, Oh Jesus, here we go, another nut loose in the library.

"Do you believe there's any correlation between Edwin Hubble's discovery that the universe was expanding and the great stock market crash, since both occurred in 1929?"

"It never occurred to me," she lied. It was an idea to which she had once actually given considerable thought but then came to her senses and dismissed as absurd. "Probably just a co-incidence," she said, trying to cut the conversation short.

He persisted, however, explaining to her that he was an expert in nothing but deeply interested in everything. Her right ear—the good one—was toward him, so she could hear him very clearly. She detected a slight, even affected, accent, and the sound of his voice was soothing and a little sinister. She sighed and promised herself that she would never again make the mistake of sitting anywhere but in a cubicle, which was effectively designed to cut out the riffraff. She was greatly relieved when he gathered up his pile of reading material and stood up to leave. As he walked away, he handed her his card, which read *Marco Trentadue, Freelance Intellectual, New York City. Spontaneous encounters only.* Marie read it, chuckled, threw it in her backpack, and expected she would never see the guy again.

During the next month Marie ran into Marco at the library several times (always dressed in the same navy-blue pajamas).

She had a feeling this was not a coincidence, but the odd little man—who was of an indeterminable age somewhere between thirty and fifty—seemed harmless enough. Their conversations were brief at first, but slowly they began talking for longer and longer periods of time—or rather Marie began talking. Marco had this uncanny way of making Marie tell him about herself, something she was definitely not used to as a journalist and a woman. With Ned Brilliant, as with most of her male colleagues, she was lucky if she got a word in edgewise. ("Don't worry," Marilyn Monroe says to Anne Baxter in *All About Eve*, "you won't bore him. You won't say a word.")

In all fairness, Marie had to acknowledge that usually she herself had an uncanny ability to make others talk. For some reason, people, even absolute strangers, often felt compelled to confess their lives to her. She didn't know why—whether it was because she asked the right questions or knew when to be silent or whether it was because she was partially deaf in one ear. Her deafness caused her to hold her head slightly to one side when someone spoke and she concentrated on filling in what she might have missed by reading lips and eyes. It appeared that she was listening with great interest and intensity to whatever was being said.

Marie thought Marco produced this loquaciousness in her because he had trained (he said) for four years in a Lacanian psychoanalytic institute in Paris. ("I don't believe in institutes, degrees, or memories, so I left," he had explained.) Often he appeared not to be listening to what she was saying. His eyes would glaze over, he'd pull on his goatee or stroke his mustache and periodically glance at his watch. Or he would conspicuously turn the pages of the newspaper (he read several every day) or quote to her from whatever book he was reading, inevitably some French theorist Marie had never heard of. (Marco always referred to the authors by their first names: "Jacques says . . . Luce feels . . . Hélène points out . . .") At other times, however, he clung to her every word as if she had the answer to the riddle of the Sphinx. Marie found all of his habits annoying and insulting, but for some reason they did not stop her from speaking to him. On the contrary, they incited her to tell him more and more about herself.

At first Marie considered Marco to be a full-blown psychopath (Peter Lorre in *The Stranger on the Third Floor*), a casualty of Ronald Reagan's social programs, which included the closing of the city's asylums (hence the pajamas), and had tried to avoid him. But with time, although Marco's awkward charm, macabre looks, and strange intelligence often gave Marie the creeps, she sometimes found herself looking forward to their meetings at the library—which were never planned. Neither had ever expressed any interest in seeing one another outside the premises of the former department store.

As she was watching the door to the Ear Inn, Marie realized she had been expecting a short, goateed man dressed in blue— i.e., Marco—to walk in, not Rex Mars. Actually, she was pretty sure Rex Mars was the guy sitting next to her at the bar who had just ordered another Jack Daniel's—his third since she arrived. She had noticed him immediately when she walked in— and not only because of his cobalt-blue alligator skin cowboy boots. He was also wearing a tight white T-shirt over a Michelangelo-worthy upper torso. Several factors had stopped her from introducing herself immediately: she couldn't quite fathom that he had arrived earlier than she; his resemblance to the photograph of him that as a teenager she had kissed nightly was minimal; she was suddenly overwhelmed by the knowledge that she would be having a conversation with someone she had once both adored and envied as Nora Mars' lover.

It was Marie's infatuation with Nora Mars, as well as her increasing sense of temporal urgency, that had made her ask *Gotham City Star*'s owner and editor in chief, Miles Brewster, if she could do a solo—research *and* write—Nora Mars obituary. She had walked into his Plexiglas-enclosed office in the middle of the floor at the *Star* the previous afternoon and said in one breath, "I've been on staff for nearly ten years now and if I get a couple of bylines a week on fascinating subjects like recycling, I'm lucky. I literally know Nora Mars better than I know my own mother. I want to do the story by myself. And frankly, it's about time."

Miles Brewster, who was referred to on the floor as "007" because of his tendency to snoop around his employees' desks, winked one of his violet-colored eyes at Marie. It wasn't actually a wink. It was a tic he had in his right eye that she had initially found very distracting. He was her boss and she was always afraid he was coming on to her, trying to establish some banal sexual subtext through eye signals. It took Marie years to figure out that he wasn't winking just at her but at the whole staff indiscriminately. Even after this discovery, however, she couldn't shake the feeling that Brewster had a thing for her.

Apart from this tic, he was a handsome sixtyish WASP. He lived on Park Avenue, owned an island in Maine, and had a voluminous collection of bow ties. Marie was sure she hadn't seen him wear the same one twice. He had a full head of snow-white hair and glowing leathery skin from a lifetime of sailing and tennis. He came from a family of bankers whom *Forbes* magazine deemed one of the richest in America, and it was common knowledge that one of his ancestors had crossed the Atlantic on the *Mayflower*.

Brewster had scandalized the family once upon a time with his muckraking ambitions, but, as he explained it, he appeased them by never slacking off on enjoying the perks of the very rich, keeping horses and helicopters at his disposal. Of even greater significance, his family soon came to realize that his private holding was a considerable asset as a tax write-off. No one but the Brewsters knew exactly how much the *Star* lost each year, but the sum was no doubt astronomical.

Otherwise, the *Star* was a huge success because it was the paper everyone loved to hate. The paper's great claim to fame lay in its oxymoronic nature. A highbrow tabloid, it contained the usual gossip, scandal, and tragedy combined with a certain *je ne sais quoi* aimed at appealing to the snob in every one of its readers. Although it had a lower newsstand price than other tabloids, it was printed on higher-grade paper and was designed with brightly colored graphics reminiscent of children's readers from the 1950s and '60s like *Dick and Jane*. The articles themselves were inevitably sprinkled with pseudointellectual references (usually added by Brewster himself). Because Brewster didn't have to answer to anyone, he could offend everyone and did so often, incurring libel suits with some regularity.

Marie stared at Brewster's winking eye, waiting for an answer to her Nora Mars obituary request.

"Time flies like an arrow; fruit flies like a banana," Brewster said out of the corner of his mouth, pretending to smoke a cigar and rapidly raising and dropping his eyebrows in a plausible Groucho Marx imitation. His little scene threw Marie off balance in a moment when she needed all of her wits to behave. Just the other day at the library she had mentioned this very same Groucho Marx quote to Marco.

A heat wave had washed over the city, and the sudden change in temperature had made her lethargic. She didn't feel like working on her philosophy of science paper and went to the magazine rack, where she ran into Marco. He had asked her when she had first heard the term "quantum mechanics."

"From Mr. Waugh, my high school physics teacher," Marie explained as she sat down to the left of Marco in one of the brown vinyl chairs in the reading area. "He was a tall, dashing, blond and blue-eyed thirty-year-old who was taking time off from his doctorate to teach public school."

Marco began reading *Time* magazine and as she talked he slowly turned its pages.

"I was a senior, and my brother, Michael, a sophomore. We were in the class together. I was dead set on becoming a cosmologist and so persisted in taking science and math classes, though I inevitably got Ds—even those were given out of pity. Michael, on the other hand, had nearly failed freshman English yet wanted to be a writer. He despised math and science but got straight As in those subjects, often without cracking a textbook. It killed me."

Marco put down *Time* and began to read *Modern Maturity* while pulling on his goatee. As usual, Marie was reviled by the gesture but she went on with her story anyway.

"I sat at the front of the class so that I could hear better and Michael sat at the back of the class so that he could read one of his science-fiction or detective novels without getting caught. It was the end of the year and Mr. Waugh had been trying to introduce the basic idea of Einstein's special theory of relativity. Every so often he would tell the class that today he just wanted to 'bang around some ideas' and that nothing they discussed would be on the exam, so they should relax and have fun with some crazy concepts. Of course, to the students this translated into free period and rarely did any kind of idea-banging occur.

"On one of these days, written large across the blackboard was the sentence 'Time flies like an arrow; fruit flies like a banana.—Groucho Marx.' Mr. Waugh explained how time, like language and meaning, was relative to its context. Einstein, he told us, had changed our whole concept of time. Time was actually the equivalent of motion, an arrow that could go any which way in space, not necessarily only toward the future. Einstein had shown that the three dimensions of space (height, width, depth) and the one dimension of time were a four-dimensional whole, which was soon labeled the spacetime continuum. Mr. Waugh said that according to Einstein's theory, time slows down to a near stop as it approaches the speed of light. This means that different observers moving at different speeds will disagree as to whether one event occurs before or after or at the same time as another event. One constant of special relativity is that nothing can go faster than the speed of light."

Marco had put down *Modern Maturity* and was staring fixedly at Marie's mouth as if each word were a precious drop of some magical elixir.

"Aware that he was losing the attention of his students, Mr. Waugh tried another tactic: 'In other words, if things could go faster than the speed of light and then slow down, it would mean we could travel into the past and, say, prevent our obnoxious little brothers from ever being born.'

"All eyes were once again on Mr. Waugh. He then described how spacetime could be warped by gravity and speed, the most extreme example of which is a black hole. By linking two black holes, a tunnel through spacetime called a wormhole would be created, allowing a traveler who entered at one end to exit at the other in a different time and place in the universe.

" 'Sounds like *Star Trek*,' my brother said skeptically.

" 'Yes, only we could never really do it because of a phenomenon called spaghettification,' Mr. Waugh responded.

" 'You mean, like, pasta?' asked Joe Moon, looking confused.

" 'Yup. In a black hole the gravitational field is so intense that any astronaut who went near a black hole would be stretched and squeezed so that he looked like a piece of spaghetti.'

" 'A cosmic anorexic,' said Veronica Sheehan brightly.

"Mr. Waugh then became entirely lost in his own world as he scribbled square roots of negative numbers on the blackboard. And that is when he mentioned quantum mechanics, Stephen Hawking, and the Big Bang. He said the universe was probably an infinite quantum mechanical time warp in which one man's microsecond is another man's forever. At the time, Stephen Hawking had yet to become famous and the Big Bang was a theory far from being generally accepted as it is now. My Mr. Waugh was in the vanguard of theoretical physics," Marie sighed. "So I raised my hand and, to show that I had been listening, asked him what he meant by the term 'quantum mechanics.' "

" 'Quantum mechanics,' he answered, 'describes the behavior of our world's microscopic matter, and is probably the strangest thing human minds have ever had to grapple with. In the quantum world all rules are only probabilities and nothing is real; the best you can hope for is a set of delusions that agree with one another.' "

Marie looked over at Marco, who appeared dazed or awestruck, she wasn't sure which. "No one in the class was listening," she went on, "except for me, and I hung on his every incomprehensible word while wondering if this was what it felt like to be in love."

"So what you're saying, then," Marco began a little breathlessly, "is that according to the laws of physics time has no meaning, the future and the past don't exist? They are an illusion, a creation of the human psyche?"

"I'm not saying it. Mr. Waugh said it, or something like it," Marie answered, feeling a little exasperated for no good reason. "Remember, I didn't even finish one year of graduate school and that was in philosophy, not physics. But from what I understand, in the universe time is perceived as having the following arrows: thermodynamic time, in which everything is increasing in entropy or evolving toward disorder; psychological time, which consists of memories or projections; cosmological time, which will be described with the definitive discovery of either the expansion or the contraction or some other inconceivable state of the universe." Embarrassed by having gone on for so long, she added, "The reality is that I have just wasted a good deal of time." She stood up, immediately feeling like the Toronto Tower, and hurried off back to her cubicle.

Staring at the Empire State Building from Brewster's office, Marie was hoping for a lightning bolt of inspiration to strike her with the meaning of Brewster's Groucho Marx impersonation. But all that came to her was the memory of her brother, Michael, turning to her as they were leaving Mr. Waugh's physics class that day back in high school, and saying: "Time, time, what is time? The Swiss manufacture it, the French hoard it, the Italians squander it, the Americans say it's money, the Hindus say it doesn't exist. You know what I say? I say time is a crook."

"Peter Lorre in *Beat the Devil,* 1954," she had responded proudly, but as for the Groucho Marx quote Miles Brewster had just flung at her, she had no idea which movie it came from and that annoyed her. It also annoyed her that he wasn't taking her seriously, that he was responding to her request with a line of slapstick. She decided not to say anything to Brewster, to remain silent. Although it was counterintuitive, she had found during interviews that silence was sometimes the most effective tactic. Most people are desperate to fill a silence and will often surprise you with unexpected information if you just leave them alone with their thoughts long enough.

Brewster took his loafered feet off his desk and sat up, winking. "Look, the point is: time is relative. To me you are, careerwise, still a babe in arms. Frankly, Marie, the reason I haven't assigned you more solo pieces is that I just don't believe you've really decided yet that tabloid journalism is for you. I always sense that you're holding out for something else, something better. I'm not sure you want it badly enough, that you're bloodthirsty enough, to be any good at it."

"If you want me to beg, I will," Marie said, feeling like a trapped animal that had just been skinned alive. Her silence strategy had certainly worked—Brewster had given her more unexpected information than she wanted. She wondered if she *would* beg.

"Okay," Brewster said, fiddling with his purple bow tie.

"You really want me to beg?" Marie asked, feeling sick.

"No. Do the story. I'll tell Edith but you deal with Abe, who will balk. Just remember, Marie, this is big, so don't fuck it up."

Marie smarted at Brewster's automatic assumption that she wouldn't do a good job. How had he gotten this low impression of her? She always tried to be efficient, thorough, and helpful. And it had all been so useless. He had seen right through her—all her helpfulness just a way to anticipate the inevitable, a way to bring on the demise of her own career before it even started.

("There is nothing more efficient than death." Nora Mars, *Two Deaths*, 1966.)

Marie looked through the Plexiglas at the *Star* staff bustling with activity. She knew they made an extra show of appearing busy when Brewster was in his transparent office. Edith Quick, the obituaries editor, would be thrilled at Marie's assignment. She was always urging Marie to take more initiative and to demand credit when credit was due. Abraham Singh, the entertainment editor, was a little more problematic, as he was extremely territorial and very moody. But she wasn't actually that worried about Abe, because he owed her. She'd practically written his last five articles.

"I want a scandalous send-off for the scandal queen," Brewster said, the sound of his voice reminding her that she had just demanded and been given the story of her dreams. "You do like scandal, don't you, Marie?"

Brewster winked another ambiguous wink. While trying unsuccessfully to suppress a blush, she speculated about the evolutionary purpose of embarrassment.

"Start with the ex-husbands," he went on. "I believe the third husband, the crooning boy wonder Rex Mars, lives in Brooklyn."

Even hearing his name made Marie swoon a little inside.

For a split second she felt the full force of her teenage crush, how she had listened to his debut album, *She's an Hourglass*, incessantly, how she had tormented herself over every last word in the letter she wrote to him asking for his autographed picture. And the ecstasy she experienced when she received in the mail his signed photo. He was twenty years old when he and Nora Mars, then thirty-six, married in 1973. Marie was thirteen at the time and she remembered thinking that she was closer in age to him than her beloved movie star was.

As Marie was about to introduce herself to Rex Mars at the Ear Inn, she considered how much of her anticipation, which had increased with the ticking of the clock, was a remnant of her thirteen-year-old self and how much was to be attributed to her ambition to get a good story out of him for the *Star*. She was also wondering what toll twenty-six years had taken on her once-adorable Rex Mars when, like the flutter of a moth, she felt the tickle of breath in her left ear—the deaf one. She jumped, nearly falling off her barstool, napkin—with the calculations of her wasted life—and pen tumbling to the floor. Looking around to see who had been whispering to her, she was hit with the hot smell of whiskey breath.

"Don't you know," Rex Mars said provocatively, "that writing on napkins in a bar is a cliché?"

Marie pulled her eyes away from his sparkling green ones in order to take in his brown curly hair, his two-day beard, his rippling upper-body muscles, and his swagger (even though he was sitting). His body had endured the twenty-six years rather well, but his face, though still dazzling, was puffy and lined and indicated that he had a life, for better or for worse, that consumed him.

She sat back on her barstool and was about to tell him who she was when he said, "You know who you look like?"

Olive Oyl, Shelley Duvall, a tall Talia Shire on a good day. Marie braced herself.

"You look just like Clara Bow or Louise Brooks, or no, I've got it, Cyd Charisse," he said with perfect incredulity, "when she dances with Gene Kelly in *Singin' in the Rain*."

It was a compliment of the highest order, a perfect-pitch lie, which meant he wanted something. He either wanted to pick her up or, knowing she was the journalist who was to interview him about his ex-wife, butter her up, win her sympathy. Little did he know that there was no need. Marie was attractive (in spite of her height) but she knew she wasn't beautiful. She'd been told too often how gorgeous her eyes were ("onyx pools flecked with gold hidden beneath the long shadows of thick eyelashes," Ned Brilliant once said) in lieu of generalized appreciation. She decided on the spot, however, that her present Clara Bow black bob hairstyle was staying.

While the bartender, a young Asian woman, poured another whiskey into Rex Mars' glass, he said, "I'm supposed to be meeting a journalist. Wouldn't it be a coincidence if you and she were the same person?"

In a genuinely fascinated voice, Marie said, "You're Rex Mars," and in total calculation, placed her hand on his arm for fifteen seconds before withdrawing it.

Ideally, she did not want to conduct the interview at the bar. Glancing around at the layout, the possibilities were three tables by the storefront window and four more tables in a dark back room area on the far side of the counter. The only other customer in the bar, a seventyish blonde with a large mole just to the left of her mouth, was sitting at one of the front tables. Marie suggested they move to the table next to the platinum blonde. Rex said he preferred one of the tables in the back— "it will be more intimate."

As Rex stood, Marie noted with pleasure that he was taller than she, which led to a momentary fantasy about a day in the future when she would be telling her children about the afternoon long ago when she and Daddy—former husband of the great movie star Nora Mars—met at the Ear Inn. There was no denying that "Marie Mars" had a certain ring to it. But she didn't have time to indulge in these reveries. She had a story to write. She gestured to the bartender to bring them another round, then took a small tape recorder out of her bag and clicked it on.

"So, Rex," she said, turning her head slightly to the right, her eyes resting on his pink lips, "tell me your story. Tell me how you met Nora Mars."

("Every story is a love story." Nora Mars, *Evil Love*, 1962.)

2

{ TRUTH }

"The one thing I can say in absolute honesty is that I am a liar."
—LUCIAN

"I did not have three thousand pairs of shoes,
I had one thousand and sixty."
—IMELDA MARCOS

"Your theory is crazy, but it's not crazy enough to be true."
—NIELS BOHR

Marie knew she should not be at the library. She was fully participating in what she called the shoot-yourself-in-the-foot syndrome. By coming to the library, she was undermining herself, her career. Brewster had finally given her a chance to write a major piece for the *Gotham City Star*; Rex had obliged by telling her an eminently tabloid-worthy story about Nora Mars, and here she was in the library examining her navel—or, to be more precise, reading about truth in science.

Earlier that day, after leaving the Ear Inn, she had headed straight back to the *Star*, where she immediately transcribed her interview tape and made some phone calls trying to check, as far as possible, on the truth of Rex's story. She also looked over what was in the advancer file, material she herself had written some time ago:

Nora Mars, whose film career began in the mid-1950s and spanned twenty years, stood as a mirror of the American psyche. In her early movies, when the green-eyed blonde was often referred to as "Marilyn's younger sister," she played the innocent hopeful willfully unaware of life's tragedies. She was the gorgeous girl next door whose exuberant happiness was threatened by large dark forces combining against her.

*After Marilyn Monroe's death in 1962, Nora Mars' career faltered and nearly ended after a string of films that were failures at the box office. Every time the public saw Mars' face they were reminded of Marilyn's scandal-ridden suicide and the violent loss of innocence that characterized the sixties. But in three memorable films—*Edgeware Road, Two Deaths, *and* The Downstairs Room—*released in 1966, Mars made a spectacular comeback, reinventing her persona as a tough, cynical, bruised romantic a la Lauren Bacall with the edgy intelligence of Bette Davis.*

During the 1970s, she dropped all pretense of innocence,

almost exclusively playing the role of aggressive, self-absorbed, and irresistible femme fatale. She made a series of psychological thrillers such as Southside, Geniuses, *and* The End of Sarah *and a number of neo-noirs, including* Checkmate *and* The Labyrinth. *She received an Oscar nomination for her performance in her final film,* The Diva, *which was loosely based on the movie classic* Sunset Boulevard.

But as she was getting more and more excited about the scandalous send-off for the scandal queen she was going to be able to deliver to Brewster, something about what happened at the interview with Rex Mars kept nagging at her. For one thing, he drank too much. Even though Marie knew that romanticizing alcoholics was entirely passé, she still couldn't help but find Rex's drinking sexy. He reminded her alternately of William Powell in *The Thin Man* and of Ray Milland in *The Lost Weekend:* extraordinarily charming and in need of saving. But his excessive intake of whiskey was not what was bothering her. What she couldn't quite figure out was whether or not Rex had been truly coming on to her during the interview. She was convinced that he was and just as convinced that he wasn't.

She played the interview tape several times to see if it might give her any kind of perspective on the matter. But in listening to the tape, she realized that it hadn't been so much what Rex Mars had said to her as how he had looked at her, repeatedly placed his hand on her arm, shoulder, knee, and at one point, had even rubbed his foot—cowboy boot and all—up against her leg. In fact, she concluded, someone who simply heard the tape would have no reason to draw the conclusion that Rex Mars had even been flirting with Marie, much less making multiple passes at her. So, she deliberated, did it actually happen? She was sure she hadn't entirely imagined his advances, but with no proof did it matter what the truth was?

Remembering that the Science, Industry and Business Library was open late that evening, she had abandoned the *Star* with a first draft of the story written and guiltily headed down the block to her safe haven, to the place that was inextricably connected to what she believed would solve all her life's questions: her paper on the relationship between quantum mechanics and reality.

Marco had been there as usual, dressed in his blue pajamas, reading a stack of magazines and newspapers. Marie had waved to him as she passed, heading for her favorite cubicle by the microform room. She had recently been reading Popper, Kuhn, and Feyerabend, for what Marco had come to refer to as her "quantum paper." Marie considered these guys the Groucho, Harpo, and Chico of the philosophy of science because they often argued to the point of hilarity—in their case, that there was no distinction between observation and imagination or between evidence and prejudice and that science was therefore unable to achieve objective truth. She read a couple of pages in Feyerabend in which the author stated that there was no logic to science; that scientists created and adhered to scientific theories for what were ultimately subjective and even irrational reasons; that truth itself was a rhetorical term. But her mind had quickly drifted to Rex. The interview had, in fact, begun with a lie.

"I was twenty years old when I met Nora Mars," Rex said, launching his tale. "Or rather when she met me."

"So young," Marie had responded, although at the time, to the thirteen-year-old Marie reading the tabloids, Rex Mars had seemed an adult, much more than only seven years older than she. "How old are you now?" She already knew the answer but had found that with both men and women, if she got them to articulate how old they were early on in the interview, things went a little more smoothly. It was almost as if after revealing their age, they felt they had nothing else to hide.

"Forty-two," he said with a childish grin. "At least ten years older than you."

Marie was a bit surprised, but mostly charmed, that Rex Mars was lying about his age—not to mention her own. He had married Nora Mars when he was twenty years old in 1973, which made him forty-six. Marie also lied about her age from time to time but she told people she was *older* than she was— sometimes by as much as three years. She was never sure just why she had this impulse to claim she was older except that it comforted her somehow. She was sure Marco would see it as part of her chronic need to anticipate, and she supposed it was.

She also lied about her height, which, according to a study she had read recently in the *American Statistical Association Proceedings*, was a common practice among Americans. Mostly, people added a couple of inches, whereas Marie regularly shaved off two and a half. But what psychosociologists found most interesting about the statistic was the cultural complicity in lying about stature: it is easy to visually assess someone's height by comparing his or hers to your own, yet, the study claimed, consistent lying about height appeared to be not only culturally condoned but "perhaps even required."

For the most part, though, Marie didn't go in much for lying, not because she disapproved of the practice, but because she wasn't very good at it. She could never remember to whom she'd told what lie, so it was just better to stick to the truth. The last time she engaged in the exhilarating exercise of spinning a vast web of lies, the consequence was the fifteen-year-and-counting loss of her brother Michael's trust and companionship.

"Maybe I'm forty-four," Rex Mars went on, after a large swallow of whiskey. "I've stopped keeping track."

Marie was tempted now to lie to him and tell him he looked just as he did as a twenty-year-old but she resisted. The focus had to remain tightly on his story. She had, of course, learned this the hard way ("the only way," Brewster had consoled her). In her first interviews, she had empathized with the interviewee, helped finish thoughts or sentences when the person was having a rough time, resorted to flattery to ease the tension. She came away from the meeting with a new friend, but had no quotes, no meat, to put in the story.

"What exactly did you mean," she asked, "when you said that you didn't meet Nora but Nora met you?" Marie stole a glance at Rex's left hand. The ring finger was vacant and longer than his middle finger. Asymmetrical hands, she had read in some obscure journal, indicated in men an elevated level of testosterone and a low sperm count. What was it about her particular configuration of neurons, she wondered, that made her mind retain such weird pieces of information?

"It happened like this," he said, sounding falsely cheerful. Even after all these years, Marie thought, talking about Nora Mars was probably still painful for him. She herself had always found the truism "Time heals all" to be a lot of baloney. Time just seemed to make everything more terminally diseased.

"I quit community college in Ohio and hopped a bus for New York City with my guitar and one hundred dollars. After two years, the pinnacle of my career was a gig playing happy hour in a dive called Prime Cuts in the heart of the meatpacking district. I had been performing for a few months at this club, where I was considered exotic because I was a straight white guy singing love songs. The regulars at the place were transvestites, transsexuals, hookers, johns, dykes, and dominatrixes. One evening I felt the room get quiet and tense, and I knew it wasn't the ballad I was singing that was hypnotizing the crowd. For a while I thought it was just the appearance of another undercover cop, until I realized that the energy in the room was coming from excitement, not fear."

Rex pulled a pack of Lucky Strike out of his pocket and offered one to Marie. She declined. She had always wanted to smoke but had never been very successful at it, so she gave up trying. Nora Mars had always looked spectacular with a cigarette dangling from her dark lips or balanced precariously between her long fingers. Rex lit up, then continued.

"At first, I couldn't see who was causing all the stir because the lights were in my eyes. Then when I finished the set, I got this little note written on a napkin . . ."

He paused, locked eyes with Marie, and smiled at her as if they were in on some intimate secret. She glanced over toward where she had been sitting at the bar. The napkin numerically describing her own wasted life still lay on the floor. She hoped she would never have to explain the meaning of those calculations to anyone, much less to the handsome ex-husband of her childhood idol.

Wrapping his fingers around Marie's wrist, Rex squeezed lightly, then said, "In red ink she'd written: 'Sing the next one for me and I'll buy you a drink.' "

The actress was renowned not only for her numerous marriages but also for her extramarital flings, for picking up men in bars, and for her one-night stands, and Marie, as a teenager, had scanned the supermarket tabloids for every last sordid detail about her affairs. ("How many husbands have you had?" a snide reporter once asked her. "My own or other people's?" she countered without missing a beat.) Marie always loved how Nora Mars breathed in and exhaled men like so much air, but she recalled feeling sorry for Rex when the news hit the stands that his short gasp with Nora was over—even though it had also meant he was now free to marry Marie.

At this point in the interview, Marie had realized she was essentially just riding it out. The truth of Rex's story was not at issue—for all she knew, it was a complete fabrication and that was fine by her. The problem was the story he was telling her would not be usable, because she'd heard or read various versions of it before. The story was worn out, old news. So she had decided to just be patient with Rex's rambling, and like a shrink, listen for a slip, a word out of place, an inadvertent thought that would lead, like a rainbow, to a pot of gold—which, indeed, it had.

("I never know how much of what I say is true." Nora Mars, *The Diva*, 1977.)

At her cubicle in the library, Marie had totally lost her patience with the arguments—or slapstick routines—she was reading about truth in science. She thought she'd do just as well to read a mindless magazine for a while to clear her head. Of course, as luck would have it, the only free chair in the reading area was the one next to Marco's. She grabbed a copy of *Glamour* and, against her better judgment, sat down next to him.

She noticed he was reading *Weekly World News,* and the headline of the article he was staring at was: PARK AVENUE CANNIBAL: UPPER EAST SIDE MAN EATS HIS ENTIRE FAMILY. Marie knew the story, though luckily she hadn't had to work on it. The so-called cannibal had made comestible voodoo dolls of his wife and two daughters which he had been devouring when interrupted by the building's super. The super had called the police because he was worried about satanic practices taking place in his building.

"It is a clever headline," Marie told Marco, who barely looked up at her, "and a good example of tabloid truth. The statement it makes is true but tantalizingly misleading."

"I've been thinking about truth lately," Marco said, finally acknowledging her presence, "in relation to what you told me about time—that it doesn't exist. Whether truth or time actually exists ultimately doesn't really matter. We spend our lives searching, in one way or another, for truth. Like time, the concept of truth organizes our lives, gives us a sense of meaning, and creates the fundamental notion of 'progress.' Perhaps time and truth are not real but they are crucial to our psychic survival."

She'd fled Groucho, Harpo, and Chico back in her cubicle, Marie thought, only to collide with Zeppo. Refusing to despair, she closed her magazine, sank down in her chair, and laid her head back.

"When I was about eight years old," she began, "I discovered that there were three kinds of truth—absolute truth, relative truth, and lies. I used to play a game with my father called 'Do you love me?' I would take his hand and squeeze it tightly four times, once for each word. He would respond by squeezing my hand three times for the words 'Yes, I do.' Then I would squeeze twice for 'How much?' And he would squeeze my hand until it hurt, which meant he loved me infinitely and forever. The game, which was entirely unspoken, could be played at any time: while watching TV, while in the car, while my father was talking to someone else—a neighbor, the doctor, his new girlfriend, Patricia."

Marie could hear the faint rustling of newspaper, and out of the corner of her eye she saw Marco pulling on his goatee. She contemplated telling him how much she detested facial hair on men, especially when they had the habit of playing with it. Instead, she continued her story.

"I stopped playing the game when my father announced he was going to marry Patricia and they would soon be moving back to Canada, where she was from. Every so often, he would take my hand in his and squeeze it or try to make me squeeze his, but I let my fingers go limp and tried to imagine that my hand had been amputated. As far as I was concerned, there was no longer any truth to the game."

Marco tossed the *Weekly World News* aside and picked up the *Journal of Psychoactive Plants and Compounds*.

"Then at the wedding, I was holding my little brother Michael's hand when he squeezed it tightly four times. I responded with three pulses—yes, I do—and he with two—how much?—at which point I flung his hand away and laughed at him, saying, 'I don't love you at all, stupid.' In that moment, I thoroughly despised my brother, although I also knew I loved and needed him more than anyone else in the universe. I realized then that the game was actually a very accurate measure of the truth."

Marie glanced over at Marco, who was still fiddling with his goatee and appeared entirely absorbed by what he was reading. She had no idea if he was even hearing a word she was saying.

"So since I was eight years old I have believed the following: There is absolute truth—I love you infinitely and forever—which is still believed in by children and the religious. There is relative truth—I love you but it's all a matter of perspective—which, since Einstein, everyone believes in religiously. And there is deep truth—I love you but I am also lying—which few can tolerate at all."

"Deep truth?" Marco said, considerably perking up.

"It's a Niels Bohr term," Marie explained. "A deep truth is a true statement whose opposite is also true."

("I'm so in love with you I wish you were dead." Nora Mars, *The Downstairs Room*, 1966.)

Marco's journal fell from his lap as he sat up. "You're talking about quantum mechanics—about the ideas behind the Copenhagen interpretation and complementarity, Heisenberg's uncertainty principle, nonlocality, eigenstates, Bell's theorem, and the Aspect Experiment, aren't you?" he asked excitedly.

How Marco had deduced this from what she was saying, Marie hadn't a clue. But ever since he discovered that Marie was writing about the philosophy of science, he had indulged in the annoying habit of trying to make analogies between everyday life and science. It was particularly bothersome to her because she had a similar tendency.

"Whoa. Slow down. Talk about neurotically anticipating. But in a sense, if you stretched the imagination to its limits, you're right: some quantum mechanical metaphor might be gleaned from my story. For example, it wasn't actually Einstein's theory of special relativity that put the nail in the coffin of objective truth," she extrapolated. "In many ways special relativity upholds the Newtonian clockwork universe. Einstein's multiple clocks are just much more accurately descriptive of our world than Newton's one. It was, in fact, quantum mechanics that forced scientists to seriously consider truth as something subjective, highly ambiguous, even paradoxical."

"You mean because of Heisenberg's uncertainty principle?" Marco asserted somewhat uncertainly.

"In part. Science has always been about measuring things accurately, and Heisenberg proved that it is physically impossible to specify the exact position and exact momentum of a particle simultaneously, thereby challenging one of the pillars of scientific method. But quantum mechanics says that nothing is true except the betting odds. Or that everything has a probability of being true."

"As in, given enough time and a typewriter, a monkey will eventually type out the entire opus of Shakespeare," Marco clarified.

"Yes, that, too, would have a numerical probability." Marie went on. "Another fundamental axiom of quantum theory most famously known as the observer question is that no elementary phenomenon is a phenomenon until it is a recorded phenomenon."

"As in, if a tree falls in the forest and no one sees or hears it, it didn't really fall?" Marco asked. Marie wondered if she would ever know Marco well enough to tell him to lose the goatee.

"Yup. So with quantum mechanics scientific truth becomes, on a particle level anyway, uncertain and subjective. Einstein couldn't stand the whole idea. He never fully accepted quantum mechanics, declaring that 'I shall never believe that God plays dice with the world.' He was a hidden-variable man. He always held out for the possibility that there was a hidden variable to quantum mechanics that would explain away these conundrums. Time has proved Einstein right in many of his predictions, but the opposite has been true for his belief about quantum mechanics. The more time passes, the more quantum theory is proved to be the most accurate description of our physical reality."

"Does that mean that if quantum mechanics is right, special relativity must be wrong?" Marco asked, surprising Marie by how closely he was following what she was saying.

"Not necessarily. But Bell's theorem mathematically demonstrates that if quantum mechanics is valid, any two particles once in contact will become 'entangled' and continue to influence each other, no matter how far apart they may subsequently move, which, of course, violates special relativity because it would mean that the particles have some sort of faster-than-light communication. This phenomenon is called nonlocality because it is independent of space and time, like consciousness or information."

"Fantastic," Marco said, his Peter Lorre eyes wide. "You're . . . it's simply fantastic."

Marie blushed and opened *Glamour* to an article entitled "Drinking and Your Love Life: Men and Women Get Honest." She had gone way out of her depth with Marco and felt embarrassed for having pretended to know anything more about quantum mechanics than even the bare rudiments. And why had she told *him* about the game she used to play with her father and the incident with Michael at the wedding? She thought about how hurt Michael must have been when she maliciously tossed away his hand.

Marie thought of Rex Mars' asymmetrical hand and calculated that the probability of her ever holding it, even squeezing it four times, had a few hours earlier gloriously increased. Or had it? Her encounter with Rex Mars brought up the observer question: since no one had witnessed their meeting and since what he had said on the tape recorder was ambiguous at best, did Rex actually make a move on her or were they still in the realm of myriad possibilities?

"With Nora Mars, was it love at first sight?" Marie had asked Rex at some point during the interview.

("I'm all for love at first sight. It saves a lot of time." Nora Mars, *Shadows of the Heart*, 1967.)

Rex had flashed her that knowing conspiratorial beam again that said, *Love at first sight is what happened when I saw you at the bar writing on a napkin.* But what he articulated was: "It took a while for me to actually see her because of the lights in my eyes. In fact, at first I thought she was just another transvestite putting me on, but I guess you could say that when I realized it was *the* Nora Mars sitting at a table right in front of me, holding me with those tantalizing green eyes, I had pretty much fallen head over heels."

Rex paused and stared at Marie with his own mesmerizing (and also green) eyes—the effect was not lost on her—then continued. "So I went and sat down with a movie star at a rickety old table in that smelly, grimy fringe club and she proceeded to quite literally drink me under the table." He took another long swallow of whiskey followed by a short tug on his cigarette. "I have no idea what she was wearing because all I saw was cleavage, and like an infant my one goal in life was to dive in and suck."

Besides his elevated testosterone, Marie thought, Rex must also have inherited a swagger gene. She resisted looking down to assess for the millionth time her own cleavage potential, deciding once again it simply depended on who was looking. Objectively speaking, however, she did have a stunning collection of bras.

"How old was Nora at the time?" Marie asked, again knowing the answer but wanting to probe the age-difference question to see if anything was left to be discovered there. While doing background research, Marie had come across tabloid headlines from the time of Nora and Rex's marriage: SUPERSTAR ROBS THE CRADLE; SHE'S OLD ENOUGH TO BE HIS MOTHER; and FEMME FATALE'S THIRD HUBBY IS FOUNTAIN OF YOUTH. The overwhelming negative press that had gone on throughout the country for weeks had drawn only one retort from the movie star, which she made to reporters in Los Angeles outside the premiere of *The End of Sarah:* "Your jealousy is delicious."

"She was thirty-six," Rex answered, scrutinizing Marie. "But she could have been ninety-six for all I cared."

Before she could stop herself Marie blurted out, "Siberians and Eskimos don't believe you have earned the status of being called old until you have reached the age of ninety."

Quite a bit of random information percolated in Marie's brain at all times. Mostly, she kept it to herself, but sometimes when she was nervous, as she was now in the presence of the gorgeous Rex, out popped some tidbit to embarrass her. She was mortified. Did she have to shove her obvious lack of sophistication down Rex's throat? He was gazing at her with bemusement as if he found awkward attempts at flirtation charming.

"So where was I?" Rex asked, stubbing out his half-smoked cigarette. "Oh, yeah. Then Nora challenged me to play Roaming Bacchus. It's a drinking game where you drink your way through all the cocktails you can name."

All of this information continued to be familiar to Marie—she knew all about Nora and Rex playing Roaming Bacchus. The story had been fed to the tabloids at the time of their marriage and Marie had even raided her mother's liquor cabinet, making Michael play the game with her until they were doubled over the toilet vomiting. She also knew what was coming next—champagne in the morning to kill the hangover; a quickie marriage; a hastily launched career as heartthrob crooner catering to the teenybopper crowd. She debated again if she should interrupt him or just let him roll. She was determined to do a good story, to prove to Brewster just how bad she did want to be a star reporter for the *Star*.

Logorrhea (a Ned Brilliant word) was actually quite common with interviewees. Once they got going, they often didn't shut up. They wanted to tell you their life story, their sister's life story, their second cousin twice removed's life story. They wanted to itemize every injustice and record every tiny regret ever felt. At some point, you simply had to turn it off. "Crack 'em open, get the booty, get away," Ned had advised her. Rex Mars' monologue, however, wasn't the usual spontaneous spilling of guts. This was prepared. This was rillettes. Marie vaguely recalled reading not long ago in the *Post* that Rex Mars had sold his autobiography to a major publisher for a sum in the high six figures.

"I don't remember leaving the bar," Rex continued. "The next thing I do remember is hearing the pop of a champagne bottle and opening my eyes to a sun-flooded apartment over-looking Central Park. I then saw Nora Mars, more stunningly beautiful than ever in a pearl-gray satin peignoir, sucking up the bubbly white foam. The first thing she said to me was, 'Drink up, before you throw up,' and when I shook my head, she came over to me, tipped my head back, poured champagne in my mouth, and said, 'Trust me.' It took her three days to cure me of my hangover, champagne being her medicine of choice. When I was back on my feet, I learned that her agent had booked me gigs all over town, promising club managers that Nora would make an appearance for at least one of the shows. And I cut my first album, *She's an Hourglass*, in less than a month—all produced and paid for by my fairy godmother, Nora Mars. I was soon presented with her pre-nup, which I happily signed—I would take her last name in exchange for lifetime financial support—and we were married at City Hall. Our witness was the county clerk. Nora's sister had refused to come and my parents never leave Ohio. We were divorced six months later and I doubt during all that time if either of us was ever sober for very long."

Marie took a sip of her beer while trying to stave off her disappointment. All of this news continued to be far too laundered. She needed something no one knew about Nora Mars, something scandalous enough to make the dead rise, since for more than twenty years the diva had been virtually defunct as far as the tabloids were concerned.

When Nora Mars turned forty, she had bowed out of show business and quietly started her own private investment banking company called In Mars We Trust. No one knew how much she had made but the rumors labeled her a multimillionaire. She was spotted on several different occasions with George Soros and Warren Buffett. But the world of high finance was really only sexy to those who were in it—unless one of them failed big-time and then everyone got interested because everyone can relate to failure.

Marie glanced over at her fallen napkin and considered if she should add to her calculations all the hours she wasted tracking down stories that went nowhere or turned out to have about a fifteen-minute shelf life. She turned back to Rex and was struck once again by how handsome he was. She decided that even if all came to naught, a couple of hours with such a good-looking man couldn't be a total wash.

"So, Rex, when is your autobiography being published?" she asked.

Rex smiled and said proudly, "Soon. And if Nora dies, probably even sooner. The story I just told you is from Chapter One. What do you think?"

"Not bad. Did you write it yourself?"

He looked offended. "You know," he said, "I always wanted to be a writer as well as a musician. As badly as things turned out with Nora, she afforded me the chance to do both."

"When did you last see Nora?"

"Nineteen seventy-three."

"You never saw her again after you were divorced?"

"In the papers, on TV, her signature on my alimony check. She wanted nothing to do with me," he said with genuine sadness—and this is when he had rubbed his foot up against Marie's calf.

She ignored the gesture and moved her legs. She was worried that Rex was becoming very drunk. During the telling of his story he had knocked back a couple more bourbons. She knew he must be plastered but she could also see that aside from the glassy eyes and the thickish tongue, he was actually a very practiced drunk. He had trained his charm never to abandon him and his speech to remain clear. With those two things in place, he could live out his life in oblivion and no one would bother him about it.

"I believe I've got everything I need," she said, clicking off the tape recorder and knowing she'd gotten a big fat nothing. Maybe she'd try a second interview if Nora Mars managed to hang on for a while. In the meantime she'd have a crack at the other ex-husbands. "I'll just settle up at the bar."

"I hope I was helpful," he said, staring into his empty glass. "Say, I have to confess I never read the *Gotham City Star*. What else do you write about besides dead celebrities?" It was obvious to Marie that he didn't want her to leave—and there was a gargantuan part of her that wanted to stay and see where this flirtation would lead—but she had a story to write. And she suspected his true motivation for wanting her to stick around could be simply explained by the fact that no one likes to drink alone. Still, she wasn't sure how to answer his question. Was she going to tell him that she was mostly a researcher, a fact-checker, a rewrite man? Was she going to tell him that her editor in chief believed she didn't have enough desire, whatever that meant, to be a really good journalist?

"Dead babies," she answered. "My last story was about a dead baby." It was the truth. Her last signed article—one she was particularly proud of—was about an upper-middle-class New Jersey girl who gave birth in the bathroom at a prom and drowned the infant in the toilet. The story broke late on a Saturday night and no one was in the office. Brewster sent her out, let her write up the first article, then gave the follow-ups to Raquelle Goode, a veteran journalist at the *Star* who wrote about "women's issues." Marie was still livid about it.

"Oh, how sad," he said, his head nodding, whether in sympathy or from alcohol it was difficult to tell. "You know, when Nora was a teenager she had a baby who died."

"How awful," Marie said, easing back into her chair. Her Nora Mars had given birth? The same Nora Mars who said, "I love children, especially when they cry, because then someone will take them away"? She quietly clicked the tape recorder back on and adjusted her head for maximum hearing. Prod with a question or wait, she debated.

Marie knew Rex could be about to make a big mistake. She knew because her whole body was tingling with excitement. He was about to tell her something that he shouldn't, a scoop, a wad of never-before-revealed exclusive information that a publishing house had paid a mega-advance for. And Rex was going to give it to her, to Marie, because she was deaf in one ear, because she wanted it bad enough, because it was time, because in vino veritas. Wait, Marie's instinct told her. Trust the silence.

"She told me about it just before she kicked me out. It was one of the few times I ever saw her sober," he began. "I woke up and it was evening. She was sitting next to me on the bed sobbing. 'I had a son once,' she said, 'and if he had lived, he would be your age.' I sat up and put my arms around her but she pushed me away. 'I killed him,' she said. 'I had to. He was barely a few days old and he was lying in my bed at home. I took a pillow just like this one and pushed it down over his little prune face. He barely even struggled, as if he knew that what I was doing was right and good. I pushed my face into the pillow so that only feathers and cloth were between my lips and his. I stayed there until he couldn't breathe. I fell asleep on top of him.'"

Marie had stopped breathing herself. This was too good to be true, the real McCoy, pay dirt. And all because she had done something she almost never did—told him something about herself. Rex suddenly had an absent look in his eyes. Marie needed to be with him wherever he was. It was her turn to touch him. She reached over and lightly placed her fingers on the back of his hand.

"Nora was shivering as she spoke, unable to catch her breath," Rex continued, and Marie surreptitiously let out a sigh of relief. "I told her she didn't have to go on, but she did anyway. She told me that when she woke up, she removed the pillow from over the infant's head, and I swear to you I will go to my grave remembering her description of that baby. She said that his skin was faintly yellow and his eyes were blank and hard like a doll's. She pushed the lids shut but they popped back up. She turned him over on his stomach so she wouldn't have to look at him, his little body floppy and compliant. Then she kissed the back of his head, her breath causing his silken hair to part and flatten against his skull like wheat in a field. The only heat she felt was from her own lips. Very soon after she told me that story, I was out on the street and never spoke to her again."

"Rex," she said, leaning toward him, "that was a very powerful and moving story." She considered thanking him for "sharing it" with her but couldn't quite get the words out. She wanted, rather, to get out of the Ear Inn before he realized what he had given her, before he started begging her not to use it, crying that his publisher would kill him. Marie had hit silver. If she could just find a speck of corroboration, the story would turn to gold. And if it were hers exclusively, she would be talking platinum.

"Rex, I need to know if you have been contacted by other

journalists," she said as the bartender arrived with another drink. Rex grabbed for it too quickly and knocked it over onto the table.

"I haven't told that story to anyone but you," he said as if she were the only woman in the galaxy.

"Can I call you?" Marie said, sincerely hoping she would be able to muster enough willpower to walk out of the Ear Inn and away from Rex Mars in the next few seconds. "There may be some follow-up questions," she clarified, giving him her card, which had her office, home, and cell numbers.

As she paid the tab, her eyes landed on the napkin with her wasted life on it. She started to lean down to pick it up but then thought better of it. After all, she realized, emerging from her meeting with Rex Mars into a balmy and strangely warm afternoon, she hadn't wasted her time in the least.

On the other hand, she had certainly been wasting her time reading *Glamour* and talking to Marco in the library when she should have been pursuing the story of her career. She looked over at Marco's chair. She vaguely remembered that a little while ago he had gathered up his papers and magazines and wandered off. She saw that he had forgotten to put back on the rack his copy of the *Journal of Psychoactive Plants and Compounds*. She wondered if Marco had a drug problem.

Rex definitely had an alcohol problem. He might never have told her about Nora Mars' dead baby if he hadn't been drinking—and a lot. It then occurred to her that Rex's story might not be true. It was a little suspicious that Marie mentions a dead baby to Rex and all of a sudden Nora Mars has one, too. But what possibly could have been his motivation for telling her that story? She closed *Glamour* and glanced at the lead header: "Your Most Intimate Info: 5 Secrets to Spill to Bring Him Closer." Was the story part of his seduction routine? Even worse, if the story was true, how did she feel about the fact that Nora Mars had committed infanticide? Too many interrogatives, she told herself. The bottom line was that Brewster was going to love it. She could already imagine his finagled headline: DIVA MAKES DEATHBED CONFESSION: I KILLED MY BABY. There was even a remote chance the story could score her a front page.

Marie's excitement, however, was accompanied by an equally charged sense of dread. If she wrote the article, using a story that might well not be true, she would effectively transform a national female icon into a megalomaniacal baby killer. She imagined Brewster winking a Morse code message: *How bad do you want it, Marie?* What was "it"? she asked herself. Fame, fortune, immortality, immorality, or simply a decent raise and a promotion after ten years on the job?

She began a litany of rationalizations: if she didn't tell the story, someone else would; given her adoration of Nora Mars, she would tell the story more sympathetically; was she just going to walk away from potentially the biggest break in her career because of some flimsy sense of morality? Ned Brilliant wouldn't question himself for a microsecond. Perhaps Marco had a point—all this anticipation of what the future could bring was causing her to get in the way of herself.

Back at her cubicle she gathered up her books and papers. She glanced at the last note she'd taken from Feyerabend—"a scientific theory is an act of creation as profoundly mysterious as, say, the Mona Lisa." As far as the truth of Rex's story was concerned, she worked for a tabloid and tabloids were all about pushing the boundaries of truth. Hadn't Marco pointed out that it was the search for the truth, or the absence of truth, or some impossible definition of truth, that drives us on? As she left the library and headed back to the *Star*, she decided that truth itself might just be beside the point.

3

{ BEAUTY }

"Everything you see, I owe to spaghetti."
—SOPHIA LOREN

"Beauty is a mystery. You can neither eat it,
nor make flannel out of it."
—D. H. LAWRENCE

"It would be a sad situation if the wrapper were
better than the meat wrapped inside it."
—ALBERT EINSTEIN

Marie was going to be late. She was driving eighty miles an hour up the Henry Hudson Parkway in a cream colored 1959 Chevy Impala convertible with a red leather interior, the same car Nora Mars drove in *The Reckoning*. She was heading for Hopewell, a small working-class town in the northwest corner of Connecticut and birthplace of Nora Mars. Hopewell was where Nora escaped from when she was sixteen and where her sister, Maud Blake, still lived.

Unlike her brother, Michael, who was obsessed with cars, Marie had always thought of them as nothing more than a means of transportation. But driving that Chevy Impala convertible with its bat wing rear fenders and cat's eye taillamps up the highway, passing trucks and receiving admiring honks and stares, made her reconsider her indifference to cars. Surrounded by all that handsome metal, Marie felt beautiful. Usually her height, her prominent cheekbones, and her wide mouth made her feel awkward and clownish, but seated in what amounted to motorized romance cruising down the road, she envisioned herself as striking, sophisticated, and seductive.

Beauty is as beauty does; beauty is only skin-deep; beauty is in the eye of the beholder—Marie didn't buy any of the clichés. She believed there was an objective hierarchy of beauty and if you were near the top of the scale life was better. There was also subjective beauty, the kind described by the song lyric "You are so beautiful to me," and that kind had its merits—but it was nothing in comparison to the beauty that was so intense, carried such an aura, that in a crowd the bearer of that beauty was easily identifiable to all.

Once, waiting to see Catherine Deneuve in a revival of *Belle de Jour* at the Paris Theater, Marie found herself sitting next to Paul Newman. His eyes were an icier blue, his face more arrestingly handsome, in real life than on the screen—or at least that is how it felt. Perhaps she wasn't actually seeing him, but rather a composite of her favorite roles he played: Brick in *Cat on a Hot Tin Roof,* Fast Eddie in *The Hustler,* and Luke in *Cool Hand Luke.* In any case, although she was dying to just say hello, to tell him how much she loved his movies, she was so intimidated by his beauty that she said nothing. When the movie (in which the ravishing Catherine Deneuve wore the most incredible outfits) was over and Paul stood up to leave (he was very short), Marie remained glued to her seat until she was sure he had left the theater.

Movie stars who went on about how beauty was a handicap, how they never knew if people liked them because they were talented or because they were beautiful, were intolerable to Marie. As if their beauty weren't integral to who they were, who they had become. It was like making the argument that a strawberry isn't inherently red, it simply reflects light at wavelengths that our brains collectively interpret as red. Our perceptions, then, that a strawberry is red and that Gene Kelley is a knockout are really just mass delusions. It was an antirealist argument for a mind-dependent reality—a way of reasoning she abhorred and one that reminded her of Marco.

Marie tended to side with the evolutionary psychologists who claim that beauty has survival value and that sensitivity to beauty is a biological adaptation governed by brain circuits shaped by natural selection. Marco had told Marie not long ago at the library that such an argument was hogwash, that beauty is a purely social construction. As evidence he cited an episode of *The Twilight Zone* in which a beautiful blonde is deemed an outcast on her planet and forced to go through cosmetic surgery because in the eyes of her fellow aliens she is hideously ugly.

("There is nothing more wasteful than an ugly man." Nora Mars, *The Reckoning*, 1959.)

"One could easily make an antievolutionary argument," Marco said, getting riled up, "about beauty as a destructive force. For example, $E=mc^2$ is by all accounts one of the most stunningly gorgeous equations of all time and yet it led to the atom bomb. And of course the poets, from Sophocles to Yeats and Rilke, were terrified by the power of beauty. Dostoyevsky quaked before beauty, claiming it to be an awful thing, an unfathomable riddle, where all contradictions exist side by side."

Marco had apparently thought about this subject at length, and Marie suspected it was because he was short. He had even devised a theory he called the theory of mutual good looks.

"Absent mitigating factors like money and power, people inevitably couple with their physical equals, their beauty equivalents," he explained.

"A silly theory," she responded. "First of all, we don't live in a vacuum, so why bother to talk about 'absent mitigating factors'? Second, what about the opposites-attract theory, Jack Sprat and his wife, or . . ."

"You and me, tall and short?" he asked.

"I wasn't exactly thinking of that example," she said, "but sure."

"My theory still works," he said, placing *Brandweek* back on top of his stack of magazines. "It encompasses the mitigating factors as well as the opposites-attract theory. You don't have to look like your partner, although that is the usual scenario; you just have to be equal in physical beauty. If, however, there isn't physical parity, it means there is some sort of miti-gating factor: he's rich, she's beautiful; he's powerful, she's beautiful; he's a genius, she's beautiful."

"She's rich, she's alone," Marie interrupted. "She's power-ful, her husband needs Viagra. She's a genius, who cares? Some pretty lopsided mitigating factors you've got there. A bad the-ory you consider stunning."

Marco shrugged. "I'm describing, not prescribing. By the way, did you know that Kafka was tall? I always imagined that he was a little man. You can't imagine my disappointment. And Oscar Wilde was a virtual tree."

Marie sat up. "Are you saying you have a problem with tall people?"

"No more than *you* might with short people."

"I don't have a problem with short people," Marie said a lit-tle too emphatically. "I like short people. Most of my favorite actors are short. In fact, you even look like one of them . . ."

Marco cut her off. "I abhor it when people tell me I look like someone else—especially since usually it is that ghoulish creature Peter Lorre. In any case," he added, "short people are closer to the center of things."

Marie kept silent. She didn't perceive Marco as ghoulish-looking; she saw him as physically exotic, like a peacock or a sea horse. And like the eye in a peacock feather or the curl in the sea horse's tail Marco's looks were disconcerting. She did won-der why he felt the need to dress in something as bland as a blue suit. Marie often felt sorry for (most) men that they didn't get to dress up, accessorize, wear makeup, nail polish, lipstick.

Just a little lipstick could often make Marie feel a whole lot better. Men didn't have such things. True, they had ties, but how limiting they were. How many variations on paisleys, stripes, and polka dots can there be? And even the concept of the tie was inhibiting—it was, after all, essentially a rope around the neck. Of course, before the nineteenth century men dressed up at least as elaborately as women. Marie pondered how women progressively through time had come to conquer the powerful realm of beauty and adornment, and what the world would be like if men were allowed to dress up again.

Another trucker honked and Marie smiled as she passed him. She had never minded the heckling of men but was disturbed, again, at the lopsidedness of it. If she were to call out to a man on the street who she thought had nice legs or was wearing a pretty tie or even just to say a simple good morning, nine times out of ten he would think she was a slut trying to pick him up and the world would have little sympathy if the situation got ugly.

She remembered Rex Mars' sculpted muscles and admired his efforts to stay physically attractive. She then thought of Marco's theory of mutual good looks and sadly concluded that she and Rex—mitigating factors included—were simply in different categories. In any case, Rex's phone call that morning—the reason she was going to be late to her interview with Maud Blake—had placed his interest in Marie in clear perspective.

Marie had walked to work early. She left her apartment in Chelsea at seven, and although the air was cool it had no edge, so she knew it was going to be another unseasonably warm day.

It was a ten-minute walk to the *Star*, which occupied the top three floors of a prewar building on Fifth Avenue and Thirty-eighth Street—formerly the offices of *El Mundo*, whose painted logo on the side of the building was still faintly visible. Across the street was Lord & Taylor and three blocks south was the newly opened Science, Industry and Business Library. The dominant landmark, however, which Marie had stared at nearly every day for ten years from her desk, was the Empire State Building. Because of the constant proximity, Marie had developed a unique relationship with the skyscraper. She identified with its height, used it to gauge the weather, and amused herself by guessing the colors of its floodlight evening wear. For the past few days it had been wearing green for St. Patrick's Day.

At her desk, sipping her third cup of coffee that morning while admiring the Empire State Building's daily wear—beige and silver with red window-frame trimming—Marie mulled over yet again the idea that Nora Mars had killed her baby. Since the actress held top idol status in her pantheon, Marie was aware that it was difficult for her to be objective. But even taking her obvious bias into account, she was still having a hard time totally believing the story. First of all, Nora Mars just didn't fit the teen-mother infanticide profile. Usually, the girl was a shy, invisible, responsible type whose teachers, neighbors, and parents were utterly shocked that she'd had sex, much less committed murder. Nevertheless, it was possible. Nora Mars' mother had died giving birth to her, and her father, a traveling salesman for a local textile company, was rarely home. Marie recalled a line from her PROM MOM DROWNS BABY IN SCHOOL

TOILET article: "She had no one to turn to, the lonely shame of her sin driving her to kill its issue."

But more to the point, it was not that Marie believed Nora Mars incapable of such a crime, it was simply that Rex Mars' account of the infant smothering sounded too Hollywood. Marie thought of Gene Tierney in *Leave Her to Heaven* (Marie's favorite of the Technicolor noirs). Enraged that her body is being deformed by pregnancy and distraught that she can no longer wear her incredible wardrobe, Gene declares, "I hate the little beast. I wish he would die," then throws herself down the stairs in a successful attempt at self-induced abortion—giving new meaning to the term "femme fatale." Marie speculated that some version of the infanticide fantasy was probably pretty common among women, which would make the Nora Mars story even more compelling.

One person who would surely know if Nora Mars had ever given birth was Nora's sister. A quick search on the Internet turned up eight Maud Blakes, but only one lived in Hopewell, Connecticut. Marie thought better of asking Maud about her sister's dead baby over the phone, so she called to make an appointment to meet with her. The woman, indeed Nora's sister, was immediately hostile.

"I have nothing to say about my sister to the press—never have and never will—so you're wasting your time."

Ned Brilliant had once given Marie a little lecture on what a good sleaze shark should do in the hardest cases: 1. He finds out something about the person he's interviewing, some personal thing, and to gain a simpatico relationship pretends that it has happened to him, too. 2. He gets into an intellectual discussion and the person lets down his guard and says things he doesn't mean to say. 3. He gets the person angry, but this can backfire.

Marie wasn't usually worried about exploiting her subjects. She saw interviews as a mutual exploitation and often came away from a story feeling used herself. But she wasn't particularly keen on any of Ned's strategies either. Nevertheless, she thought of Brewster and the calculations on her napkin from the Ear Inn and forged ahead.

"Let me be straight with you," she said to Maud Blake. "I write for a tabloid, which means I can write just about anything I want to about your sister. *But this is personal.* What I'm really interested in here is *your* story and I'll tell you why. *I haven't spoken to my brother in fifteen years.* Now, I know that you and Nora have barely talked for over forty years and I want to know the reason why. And I want to know *your* version."

Maud chuckled and said, "So you want to know *my* version, do you? All right, I'll give you my version, but I want to do it in person. I want to see who I'm talking to."

Marie couldn't believe she had done it again—she had revealed something about herself to an interviewee—only this time she had gone even further and stooped so low as to use her brother. Her only consolation was that it had worked. Maud Blake had immediately become curious about the woman who was getting "personal" with her. She had been drawn into one of the world's most compelling turn-ons: voyeurism.

Marie, of course, had made a career out of indulging her natural propensity toward voyeurism by writing for a tabloid.

She often asked herself why people got off on spying. The nice answer was that we look into other people's lives as a way of looking into our own. The better answer was that we look into other people's lives in order to avoid looking into our own. Whatever the reason, peering into another life was an aspect of her job she loved—and often found intolerable. Frequently, she simply got too involved in her subject's life. A lot of the time, Marie enjoyed the going in, the seduction, the getting intimate with the person she was writing about, but it was the getting out, the leaving, that became problematic. Sometimes she found herself feeling lonely and disjointed long before a story was finished simply in anticipation of its being over.

"Forty-seven years," Maud said. "We haven't really been close for forty-seven years." She sounded defiant. She then told Marie to come see her in Hopewell at two that afternoon.

As Marie was leaving the *Star* on her way to pick up her rental car, Rex Mars had called. When the receptionist caught her at the elevators and told her who it was, she thought: He's calling for a date. As she walked back to her desk, taking deep breaths in order to calm her pounding heart, she wondered what she would wear.

"Marie," he said, his voice heavy with sleep or stupor or sadness, "I feel really bad about what happened yesterday."

A long silence followed and Marie felt like an idiot. She realized she had been duped by her own wishful thinking. Rex wasn't calling to ask her on a date; he was calling to try to take back his story.

Finally, Rex said, "I'd really appreciate it if you didn't use anything I said to you about Nora's baby. What I told you was not gossip, it was something else—probably the only real thing of Nora's she ever gave me."

"Look, Rex," Marie said, trying not to sound disappointed, "at this point I don't know what material I'm going to focus on, but I really can't promise you anything."

"Oh, God," he said, "I don't want that story blasted out into the world. I'm not even using it in my autobiography. You see, it's about all I have left of Nora. You've got to understand that it really *means* something to me. I don't know why I told *you*, of all people, that story. I just felt so comfortable with you," he went on, his voice softening. "It felt more like I was talking to, well, a good friend. I forgot for a minute who you were."

Marie sat down, imagined torrid sex with Rex, a white dress, children, a future, all if she would just let go of this one story. "I really can't promise anything, Rex, and right now I'm in something of a hurry."

"Marie, I'm begging you. I know you have no reason to do this for me but I'm asking you as a fellow human being."

Marie hated it when people appealed to her humanity. It was so meaningless. The division between the concept of being human and inhuman was false. What was inhuman behavior? Weren't beating, torturing, raping, unique to the human species? Over the past few weeks alone, Marie had taken runner dumps on a woman who beat her six-year-old until all of her ribs were broken and both lungs collapsed; on a man who had kept his girlfriend in a closet for six months; on a gang of teenagers both male and female who broke into a seventy-five-year-old woman's apartment, gang-raped her, then burned her with cigarettes. This stuff happened every day and there was nothing inhuman about it. It was simply unbearably human. And it sold a lot of copies of the *Star*. Marie was more than likely to use Nora Mars' dead-baby material. After she published the story, she might feel some pangs of regret for hurting Rex, but, the way she figured it, in a world of lesser evils a little regret could go a long way. But for more reasons than professional, she didn't want to alienate Rex so she told him she would give his request some thought and that she would call him later that evening.

("Try everything once, then live to regret it." Nora Mars, *Dark Blue*, 1965.)

The car rental place was a small operation on Avenue B in the East Village where the *Star* had an account. It was called High-Low Cars and specialized in luxury cars, vintage cars, and wrecks, and was owned by Brewster's doorman, who was trying to make his weakness for cars profitable. On her way there, Marie berated herself for being late, which at least felt a little novel. When she arrived—at a tiny cluttered office that smelled of coconuts—the receptionist was on the phone chattering breathlessly in Spanish while chewing a huge wad of gum.

During the first ten minutes she waited, Marie resisted giving the woman evil looks. She then began to give evil looks but to no effect. Finally, just as she was about to interrupt the woman and ask to be helped, she saw on the counter a set of keys on top of the usual contract envelope with her name, *M. Brown*, handwritten across it. She grabbed both items and headed for the car, which turned out to be the long, low, wide, and curvy 1959 Chevy Impala convertible in which she was presently cruising up the Taconic Parkway. Marie knew there had to be some mistake about the car. Brewster might have a bottomless pit of financial resources but his employees were on a very short string. He would never allow such expense account extravagance. But, unable to resist driving the same make of car Nora Mars once had, Marie had uncharacteristically opted not to investigate and was, at least for the moment, thoroughly enjoying someone's error. She wondered if Maud Blake would notice the car.

The soothingly symmetrical roadside shrubbery was marred by a sign for a state mental hospital and once again Marie thought of Marco. She realized he was getting to her, that in some weird way she was actually growing fond of him. Leave it to her, she thought, to form an absurd attachment to some loony who was also short. She reminded herself of the dread she felt whenever she saw Marco at the library. His appearance inevitably meant less time for her quantum paper, that she was going to engage with a small male social outcast against her better judgment, that she was going to tell him things she never told anyone and which he hardly even listened to. She decided she had to cut off the association before it got *too* weird. Just a few days ago, he had told her another one of his nutty theories, but this one had truly disturbed her.

"I have decided," he said, "that you and I, Marie, are actually the same person, or, if you like, opposite sides of the same person, like entangled particles."

It annoyed her that he was making such a ridiculous analogy between humans and particles, but again she had to admit to herself that she was guilty of the same offense. She had often thought of Marco as the human manifestation of a WIMP—a "weakly interacting massive particle," an exotic, slow-moving theorized particle that shuns contact with all other things. One camp of physicists believed that WIMPs were the mysterious stuff of dark matter—the unknown, invisible substance making up over 90 percent of the universe's mass and controlling its fate. And, embarrassingly enough, the day before, when she had met Rex Mars, she immediately saw him as a MACHO, a "massive compact halo object," the other predominant explanation for dark matter. These huge massive objects that hung out at the edges of galaxies ranged from the size of the earth to ten times the size of the sun, but for some reason did not emit light so could not be seen. The theories and acronyms for both WIMPs and MACHOs were devised by men, and Marie supposed it was somehow connected to the fact that the missing dark matter—the most important problem facing modern cosmology—had been imagined and predicted by Vera Rubin, a woman.

"It's a bit premature to be making analogies between particle physics and humans," Marie said, trying to gently dissuade Marco from his crazy theory. "We know so very little. For example, in the universe there are 100 billion galaxies. In each galaxy are 100 billion to 400 billion stars. Each star might have one to nine planets in orbit around it as well as trillions of meteorites and asteroids. All of this stuff comprises ten to the negative 27 percent of the total volume of the universe—that is point zero zero zero . . ." and Marie went on to say "zero" twenty-four more times, then added "1 percent. Do you realize what a relatively minuscule amount that is? And we have no idea where the rest of the matter or energy is. Unless, of course, as one theory has it, the universe is illusory. Light from the stars could bounce around a cleverly shaped universe, taking multiple paths to our eyes, so it just looks like there's a lot of stuff out there."

Marco's wide-eyed expression and almost mesmerized demeanor again made Marie uneasy. She quickly reminded him that if there was anything certain to be gleaned from modern physics, it was that the world of quantum mechanics—the theory that gave us entangled particles, but also transistor radios, the Walkman, digital watches, pocket calculators, and personal computers—could not be truly conceived of even in our wildest dreams.

Marco, however, persisted. "At some point, we were the same person, and then we were divided. Now we float around the world as two parts of the same self, although whenever anyone tries to peg—or measure—one of us, it causes both of us to collapse into definite and opposite values, no matter where we may be. For example, when someone says you're tall, I become short. When someone says I'm a relativist, you become a realist, and so on."

"That's an interesting idea," she replied uncomfortably. "But first of all, what you're talking about works for photons, not humans. Second, the polarizations of two entangled particles can also be identical, meaning they both collapse into, say, verticle positions—they're both entangled to be tall. Third, I really should go do some work on my paper."

"All right," he said, riffling through his collection of newspapers. "Tell me one thing. Has being six feet tall ever been a problem for you?"

Five feet eleven and three-quarters inches, she thought, then said, "No."

Marco started to read the *Post*.

"When I was a little girl," Marie sighed, placing her elbow on the arm of the chair and resting her chin in her hand, "I loved being tall. I felt older, more grown-up, wiser than other kids by simple virtue of my height. I was sure that the fact that I was tall meant I was destined for grand and important things in my life. This was in spite of my mother always making excuses for my height—saying that I would 'even out' in puberty, that girls developed early, that there was nothing to worry about. I wasn't at all worried. I prayed I would stay tall."

Marco looked at his watch, turned the pages of his newspaper.

"Then, soon after my father left, my three cousins—Natalie, Sarah, and Peter—started coming over to our house regularly to play with me and my brother. My cousins' preferred game was called Divorce, even though my aunt and uncle were, and still are, married. In the game, Natalie was married to Peter, Sarah was married to Michael, and I was the 'old maid' who comforted the wives after bad fights with their husbands. I didn't like the game, of course. But Natalie was beautiful—

she looked like Elizabeth Taylor in *National Velvet*—and the game was her idea and I wanted to do anything that would make her like me. If she liked me, I was convinced her beauty would somehow be reflected in me."

Marco was engrossed in his reading materials, stroking his mustache.

"One day I finally got fed up with my role and asked why I couldn't just once play a wife instead of the old maid," Marie went on. "Natalie very matter-of-factly explained to me that I could never play the wife because I was too tall. From then on, after my cousins left I often made Michael play the game with me and be my husband. But I knew I was trying to undo something that couldn't be undone. I knew Natalie had seen something in me that I hadn't been aware of: because I was tall I would never get married, because I was tall no man would ever truly fall in love with me."

Marco had shoved his stack of newspapers off to one side and was reading a book with a title in Latin. He pulled on his goatee.

"I asked my mother," Marie continued, "if she thought that in the future I might be beautiful even though I was tall. She told me that she got through the difficulties of life by relying on her belief that the world was an exquisite painting of which she was a brushstroke. At times we could only see certain dark and twisted fragments of the canvas, but each was crucial to the painting's overall transcendent beauty. Of course, I translated this answer into a simple no."

Marco closed his book and looked over at Marie. "I was just

reading Tertullian, who says that we will not chew in heaven, but that we will have teeth because without them we would look funny." He then stood up, stuffed his newspapers into his bag, and left the reading room.

Marie remembered sitting for a long time in the brown vinyl chair trying to figure out what, if anything, Marco was trying to tell her. Why would a theologian bother with the question of what we will look like in heaven? She thought of the Nobel Prize–winning physicist Steven Weinberg, who insisted that all sorts of theories could describe the physical world but only the beautiful theories were accepted and endured. "For forty years," he had written, "General Relativity was widely accepted as the correct theory of gravitation despite the slimness of the evidence for it, because the theory was compellingly beautiful." And then there was Nora Mars, who, when accepting a Woman of the Year Award from *Glamour*, had said to the audience, "My beauty is your salvation." For days afterward, the press had speculated on what she meant.

As Marie turned off the Taconic Parkway and headed for Hopewell, she wondered if Maud Blake would be as beautiful as her sister. The day itself was gorgeous—white clouds in a blue sky made brilliant by the sun. Is the world really this beautiful, she thought, staring at the stained-glass sky, or is there a beauty gene that makes us perceive it that way? What was it about beauty that we needed so badly? What was its purpose? Why a waterfall, a volcano, a butterfly, Saturn, the Eagle nebula, Paul Newman, Nora Mars?

She reflected, once again, on the two kinds of beauty: pure beauty (the kind intended by Tertullian and Weinberg), a beauty based on an aesthetic hierarchy recognizable to all humans; and relational beauty, a beauty entirely based on one's own perceptions. What intrigued Marie was the nature of the relationship between the two kinds of beauty and how their opposition to each other seemed to secure their interdependence.

She considered stopping to put the roof down on her car but decided against it. She had made good time, but still she was going to be late. Instead of reviewing her life and all its apparent failures, she began to list the disasters her lateness might cause: Maud Blake would be offended and not talk to her, Maud Blake would go out, Marie wouldn't have enough time with Maud to get anything useful out of her, and so on. Marie noticed that being late did not feel so different from being early. The particulars had changed but the self-deprecating feelings were familiar. She suspected that being on time would also feel like just another expression of the same thing.

Hopewell was a typical New England town with a Main Street crowded with small practical shops—hardware, clothing store, five-and-dime, grocery, diner. A Congregational church with a tall white steeple sat at one end of Main Street and the firehouse at the other. Maud Blake lived on Sycamore Lane in a large gingerbread Victorian painted teal blue with white trim. It was the style of house Marie's mother had always wanted to live in until she gave up all desire for material things in order to "tend to my soul" and moved to an ashram in California as soon as Michael had gone to college.

Marie pulled the car up in front of the house. For a minute she felt ridiculous, watching herself as Maud Blake might be watching her from a window and seeing an abnormally tall woman getting out of an outdated vehicle that looked more like a boat than a car. Marie realized, however, that she had other options. She put on her dark glasses, wrapped a scarf loosely around the back of her head, opened the car door, and alighted from the Impala like. . . . As she strode confidently up the front walk, the door to the house opened and Nora Mars stepped into the sunlight.

Marie stopped in her tracks, assuring herself that the glorious woman standing before her was not Nora Mars, that Nora Mars was lying in a coma in St. Vincent's, nor was this woman Nora's ghost, since Nora was not yet dead. Marie looked again—at a slim woman in her sixties, dressed in black slacks and a red cardigan, her bright blond shoulder-length hair neatly held in place by a black headband. Her face, though lined, suggested all of her sister's youthful beauty, the beauty that caused Marie to swoon while watching movies such as *Dark Blue, The Reckoning,* and *Evil Love.* And she was tall. As tall as Marie, as tall as Nora Mars. Marie tended to forget that Nora Mars was tall. In her movies she was always made to look much shorter than she was—her leading men notoriously forced to stand on stools.

"You're late," Maud said. Her lips were perfectly painted a midnight shade of red in the middle of the afternoon.

"You look just like her," Marie said, knowing immediately

that she shouldn't have. It was the kind of insensitive comment that could throw the whole interview.

("Nobody can be exactly like me. Sometimes even I have trouble doing it." Nora Mars, *The Diva*, 1977.)

"My father used to say *she* looked just like *me*. Come in."

Maud led Marie into the kitchen, a large room at the back of the house with a black-and-white-checkered Formica table and chrome-trimmed red-leather chairs. Maud gestured for Marie to sit down, then pulled an ice tray out of the freezer, along with a bottle of vodka.

Marie took the tape recorder out of her bag and asked, "Do you mind?" then surprised herself by adding, "I'm deaf in one ear and sometimes I miss things." Marie rarely told anyone about her deafness and never at a first meeting. In addition, what she had told Maud wasn't even true—Marie rarely missed anything due to her deafness. By now, it was almost second nature for her to position herself in such a way that she could hear perfectly well, but she was terrible at taking notes so she needed to use a tape recorder. In any case, she was going to have to get a handle on this new self-revelation tactic.

"Very clever of you, to use your flaw to your advantage," Maud said, handing Marie a screwdriver in a whiskey glass with a bagpiper wearing a blue kilt painted on it.

Marie took a sip from her glass and made a quick assessment: one part o.j., three parts booze. "As I told you over the phone, I am here because your sister is about to die," Marie began, aiming for the kind of harsh truth that puts a certain type of person at ease. "And I'm preparing her obituary. I have already spoken with Rex Mars . . ."

"Ah, the child groom."

"And he told me a rather harrowing story about Nora as a young woman."

"Just one?" Maud asked before taking a long drink from her glass, also decorated with a musical Scotsman.

Marie forged ahead. "He told me that Nora gave birth to a boy when she was a teenager and that she almost immediately ended his life by suffocating him."

Marie could detect no surprise, no horror, nothing but mild indifference on Maud's face.

Taking a large gulp from her glass, Marie said, "I am in the business of catering to voyeurism, and infanticide sells papers. The fact that a world-famous movie star has such a dark and ugly secret in her past is a big story. Unless you can convince me otherwise, I'm going with what Rex told me. The tabloid world is the world of antijustice, guilty until proved innocent."

Maud sighed. "I see Rex hasn't changed any. Like a two-year-old, he's still blithering and blathering whatever comes into his head without a thought for the consequences." She pointed at Marie's glass. "Is that all right?"

Marie nodded and took another long sip. The vodka's warmth, like an electric current, spread quickly from her lips to her toes. And then it came to her, what Nora Mars had meant by her comment, "My beauty is your salvation." Ugliness is just as fascinating to us as beauty. We are just as intrigued and compelled and inspired by it—we are just loath to admit it, to accept it, to tolerate what that means. Beauty, in fact, implied at all times its opposite—the ugly. We turn to beauty, set it on a pedestal, worship it, because it allows us a safe way into the ugly, the murky, the ambiguous. Beauty is a deep truth. Was that what Nora Mars meant? Marie wondered. No, she thought, that probably wasn't what she meant at all.

"You are, as you so graciously warned me, going to write whatever the hell you please," Maud said, startling Marie out of her reverie. "You have given me to understand that professional integrity demands it of you. Unfortunately, since my version of the story is not so scandalous, it may be of little interest to you." She stared at Marie with one perfectly plucked eyebrow raised.

Marie drained her glass and said, "On the contrary." She then shifted in her chair and tilted her head slightly to the right in order to hear as clearly as possible what Maud Blake had to say.

4

{ JEALOUSY }

"The ear of jealousy heareth all things."
—THE WISDOM OF SOLOMON 1:10

"What do you expect me to do? Sleep alone?"
—ELIZABETH TAYLOR

"The strongest force in the universe is not gravity but jealousy."
—ROBERT P. KIRSHNER

"There was a baby," Maud explained in her deep voice, both eyebrows arched with determination, "but he was mine, and no one ever killed him. He was given up for adoption soon after he was born."

Marie was disappointed, excited, and afraid all at once. That Nora Mars' sister had a baby out of wedlock over forty years ago was certainly not tabloid-worthy, but there was something about Maud's attitude—her sheer readiness to spill the beans—that both thrilled and frightened Marie. It was as if something inside Maud had reached a critical mass, as if years of conflicting and suppressed feelings about her sister were finally ready to burst into the open and Marie was going to be there to witness the blast. As with any explosion, it was sure to be surprising and beautiful and destructive.

"That must have been difficult," Marie said, knowing she couldn't even begin to fathom the pain of it. "I don't understand, though, why Nora would have made up such an awful story about killing her own child."

Maud shrugged her shoulders. A fat cat with orange hair jumped up on the counter and rubbed its back up against the vodka bottle. "The better question is," she said in a condescending tone that made Marie all of a sudden understand what it must have been like to grow up as Maud's younger sister, "Why would *Rex* make up a story about Nora killing her own child?"

Maud raised her left eyebrow once again and Marie realized that this expression, which appeared so intriguing and evocative on Nora Mars in the movies, was threatening and aggressive on Maud Blake in real life. Nevertheless, Marie had to admit Maud's *was* the better question, since she had heard the story from Rex, not Nora.

"I still don't get it," Marie said. "Out of all the stories Rex could make up about Nora Mars, why that one?"

"I'm no psychologist," Maud said, and Marie readied herself for the neat explanation that would only serve to obfuscate. "But where it concerns my sister, Rex has always been motivated by jealousy and revenge. You see, he was adopted and I believe he married my sister, a much older woman, in some sort of oedipal fury. He then did everything he could during their marriage to make her jealous and force her to leave him so that he could repeat the original abandonment. And now he has made up some fantastical story in which he projects himself as her murdered child." Maud paused, then added, "Of course, this is my own theory. I never discussed Rex with Nora."

All this, Marie marveled, from a woman who only minutes ago admitted to having given up her own child for adoption. It reminded her of the celebrated conundrum in physics—is an electron a particle or a wave? Niels Bohr demonstrated that it's both until someone looks. What was it about the act of observation that made an electron decide to be one thing? Why did Rex Mars decide on that particular story? Did it have anything to do with the fact that he was talking to Marie? And what was motivating Maud to talk to her?

("Jealousy is a superb motivator." Nora Mars, *No Ordinary Matter*, 1958.)

Was Maud competing with Nora for Marie's attention? After all, since her sister was in a coma, Maud's chances of winning had risen a thousandfold. Marie was intimately familiar with jealousy—it was the reason she and Michael hadn't spoken for fifteen years—and, like a black hole where all the laws of physics break down, jealousy is a place where nothing makes sense, no rules apply. But as Phaedra, Othello, and Gatsby attest, jealousy can also be a dark and twisted measure of immense love.

"Besides, isn't Rex writing a memoir?" Maud asked, taking another long swallow of her drink. "I suppose he needs something juicy to put in it."

Marie saw that Maud had a point. Money was also known to motivate. "He says he has never told anyone that story," she responded, a little too earnestly, "and that it's not in his memoir."

Eyebrow, sigh.

"Why did you put your child up for adoption?" Marie asked, reminding herself that, for the moment, the story she was interested in was Maud's story. It was crucial to a successful interview that both she and Maud believe it.

Maud gave Marie a bored, nothing-can-startle-me look, and said, "It was 1953. I was unmarried and had no offers. A girl at school had died getting an illegal abortion."

"Did your parents know?"

"My mother was dead. My father, if he even noticed, just thought I was getting plump."

"Did Nora know you were pregnant?"

This time Maud appeared genuinely startled. "Of course, dear. We *are* sisters."

For all of Maud's husky-voiced insolence, Marie sensed in those few words the devastation Maud was feeling at the prospect of her sister's imminent death. She also sensed the stirrings of a story.

"You might say that child was Nora's lucky star," Maud began, "the reason she became who she did. In high school my one passion was theater. I was the lead in all the school productions, president of the drama club, and the youngest member of the Hopewell Community Players. When I was seventeen, I was accepted by New York University's theater program and was supposed to start in the fall. But I got pregnant, so Nora went in my place." Maud picked up Marie's empty glass and opened the freezer door. Marie imagined she heard the tinkle of ice. "We looked even more alike then. Nora simply took my name." The cat jumped off the counter as Maud grabbed the bottle of vodka and upended it into Marie's glass, drowning the Scotsman. "No one in New York ever knew or even suspected we'd made the switch. The idea was that after the baby was born I would go to the city and Nora would fill me in on what I had missed. But things didn't work out that way. Our father got sick, I took a job at the mill and never made it to New York. And though my name is not Maud but Nora, as the years went by and Nora became ever more famous, everyone in town just assumed I was Maud. Only my father still called me Nora." Maud handed Marie her drink, picked the cat up off the floor and stroked him.

"That could be the libretto for an opera," Marie said.

Maud smiled. The expression in the cat's eyes—a look of cool superiority—resembled Maud's. Marie was deeply impressed by the enormous jealousy Maud must have had to contend with most days of her life. To have worked for and wanted something so badly and then to watch someone else succeed at it and get all the credit and glory that you dreamed might be yours was indeed the stuff of high tragedy.

("Thank God for repression." Nora Mars, *The Necklace*, 1960.)

Marie also knew that lost glory was a common enough phenomenon, especially in science. She'd recently read about Ralph Alpher, who, in his 1948 Ph.D. dissertation, revealed mathematically how the universe began in a superhot explosion 14 billion years ago. He predicted that the radiation from the primeval explosion still existed, it just needed to be detected. Alpher, whose idea was considered too "weird" by physicists, quit academics and took a job at General Electric working on the development of color television. Then, in 1978 Robert Wilson and Arno Penzias, a couple of radio astronomers from Bell Labs, won the Nobel Prize for their discovery of a pervasive background radiation indicating that the universe began 14 billion years ago in a superhot explosion that became known as the Big Bang. Alpher spent years trying to get recognition for his work until he suffered a nearly fatal heart attack and his family urged him to give up.

And then there was Rosalind Franklin, the British biophysicist who was the first to recognize the basic helical structure of DNA. Her research was most likely passed on to James Watson and Francis Crick by her co-worker, Maurice Wilkins, who along with Watson and Crick shared the spotlight for their discovery of the double helix and then the Nobel Prize in 1962. Marie had heard it said that Franklin was not bitter about the oversight, but she barely had time to be, as she died of cancer at the age of thirty-seven. Neither Alpher nor Franklin ever received due credit for their work.

"So your sister goes to New York," Marie said, bringing herself back from her wandering thoughts, "and becomes a big movie star, essentially in your place. You stay and live the small-town life of the martyr-spinster that was destined for her."

Maud laughed. "Do you always write in your head as you go?" She didn't wait for an answer. "I have my fits of jealousy and regret, and at times I resent Nora for her good fortune. But I also know deep in what might be called my soul that if I had gone to New York, I'd still be waitressing in some dive, waiting for my big break."

"Your magnanimity is enviable," Marie said, adding just the right tinge of irony to her voice. "I'm not sure which story is better, yours or Rex's. His has the tragic horror angle, but yours is more intriguing, bigger, plays with fate and destiny."

Maud scoffed. The cat leaped out of her arms. "Of course, in your line of work the truth is irrelevant."

"How *did* Nora meet Rex?" Marie knew she was supposed to stick to questions about Maud but she couldn't resist asking and she purposefully put great emphasis on the word "*did*" so that Maud would understand that Marie wanted *her* version of the story as opposed to Rex's.

Maud began fixing herself another drink. "As I told you, Nora and I don't really talk. But at the time my father was in the final stages of his leukemia and she would come home pretty often to visit him and would let things drop. From what I understood, Rex plagued her; followed her to every appear-ance, waited for her outside the studio, her apartment, her dentist's office. He finagled his way into parties where she was. He was relentless until finally she decided it was easier to give in than to resist. I think she married him out of pity."

"Your sister never struck me as the Mother Teresa type," Marie said, wondering if anything Rex had told her at the Ear Inn was true.

"It gets worse. As soon as they were married, he began acting like a rebellious adolescent, stealing from her, taking drugs, sleeping with Nora's secretary, her masseuse, her dog walker—often in their apartment while Nora was away on a shoot. It was a disaster. All of this is, of course, public knowledge. It came out in the divorce proceedings."

"Yeah, I know, but divorce tends to privilege the ugliest stories." Marie thought she heard the doorbell, an alarm clock, or the telephone. Maud excused herself and Marie debated if she was answering the door, the phone, or, having been reminded by her alarm, taking some crucial medication. The probability was that she was answering the telephone, and Marie became immediately suspicious that it was another journalist asking Maud to tell-all about her sister. Marie felt a strong pang of jealousy. Jealousy had a way of surprising her, grabbing her in the gut, at the most inopportune moments.

("Jealousy is true north: it tells you where you want to be." Nora Mars, *Dark Blue*, 1965.)

Marie needed to keep her cool. She needed to figure out a way to convince Maud to be loyal, not to talk to anyone else, to have an exclusive relationship with her, and Marie would never be able to pull that off if she was jealousy-ridden. For the moment, Marie felt up to it—maybe because of the vodka, maybe because even though Maud scared her, Marie also felt she could say anything to her. It wasn't because she trusted her. It was rather because Maud had such a know-it-all attitude, it oddly made taking risks with her easier. She was someone you would do anything to impress even though you knew you never could. Marie had told Maud about Michael and about being deaf— things she never revealed to anyone—in a rash effort to make an impact.

Marie had always told herself that she didn't mention her deafness to people, not because she was ashamed of it, but because she didn't want to draw attention to herself and didn't want anyone's pity. But since telling Marco about how she lost her hearing in one ear, she realized that there was another reason she never spoke of her lack of hearing: she believed that she wasn't actually deaf.

"I am 50 percent deaf in one ear because my eardrum burst when I was ten years old while on a trip to Niagara Falls," Marie explained to Marco one Saturday afternoon in the library when it was bitter cold outside and uncomfortably dry and warm inside. "Around the time of my father and stepmother's second anniversary, they decided on a whim to take us with them to Niagara Falls to celebrate. When Michael and I heard the news, we were thrilled because we rarely spent much time with our father. It wasn't long, however, before we began planning our stepmother Patricia's death, just as Marilyn Monroe had planned Joseph Cotten's death in *Niagara*. Patricia, a petite brunette with an upturned nose and a marshmallow sweet personality, wasn't so offensive that she deserved to die. My brother and I just figured Patricia's demise would allow for a greater chance of our parents getting back together, or, at the very least, of seeing our father more frequently.

Marco glanced at his watch, yawned, put down the *Wall Street Journal*, and picked up *Textile World*. Marie looked at his hands. She had noticed them many times before but each time she looked at them she was surprised by how beautifully formed they were—like hands drawn by Leonardo Da Vinci. His fingers were long and slim, his tawny skin smooth across his knuckles, his nails wide and pink and glowing. Marie, more than once, had wanted to reach out and take his hand in hers and hold it just to see what it would feel like. But she and Marco had never touched, never even mistakenly brushed against each other.

"We seriously wanted her dead," Marie continued. "But as soon as my brother and I got into my father's car I could feel the pounding in my ear that meant another ear infection. I had suffered through several that winter and refused to accept that I could have yet another. I could barely focus on our murder plans. I thought only about the growing pain in my ear, desperately trying to convince myself that it wasn't really there. No matter what excruciating level the pain reached, I decided I would not tell my father about it."

Marie took off her sweater and bundled it beneath her head. She settled deep into her chair and stared at the ceiling. "It's not that he would have been upset or angry or annoyed at my getting an earache. In fact, he was the kind of person who loved to take care of others. He worked in advertising but spent a large part of his time organizing charities and benefits, running errands for old people, reading to children in the hospital, writing letters to prisoners on death row. Long before, I had decided that I would never let my father help me. I simply did not want to be one more in the endless line of people he helped. If I told him I had an earache, it would have made everything too easy for him. He would have felt like a good man and father, helping his daughter in a time of need, and I would have been mad as hell. I didn't want his help, his sympathy, his care. I wanted to murder his wife.

"So I gritted my teeth and with a throbbing head toured the Niagara Falls Museum, put on a red raincoat and walked out onto a ledge near the top of the falls, put on a yellow raincoat and rode a boat up under the falls, went to the Canadian side and took an elevator up the spindle for a view of the falls. By then, I was in so much pain I bit through the inside of my cheek."

Marie looked over at Marco. He had *Textile World* open on his lap but his eyes were closed. She wondered if he had noticed that her lips were chapped, if it was the kind of thing he would notice.

"Then as we were wandering through Madame Tussaud's Wax Museum," Marie went on, "I collapsed onto the floor. I don't actually remember it. Michael gave me a full report later, many times over. He said I was standing in front of King Henry the VIII and his six wives when it happened. At first my father thought I had been spooked by something in the museum, but then they saw blood in my ear and called an ambulance."

Marco opened his eyes and sat up. "Madame Tussaud's is just another example of what I mean," he exclaimed. "Why do people spend large fractions of their lives watching themselves be mimicked, approximated, and distorted—be it in books, in movies, on television, in art museums, or in wax museums? Since Aristotle we have always believed that art imitates life, but maybe Oscar Wilde was onto something when he said, 'Life imitates Art.' " Marco picked up *Textile World* and began reading again. Marie continued with her story.

"Michael told me that the few hours he had to spend alone with Patricia after I was dramatically whisked away on a stretcher were sheer torture and that he would eternally hold me accountable for them. He said that she kept repeating, 'I know it's my fault. She hates me. She'd rather die than have me as a stepmother.' And Michael had to reassure her over and over again that it wasn't true, that he knew I really loved her and felt lucky to have her as part of my family.

"I stayed in the hospital for two days on intravenous antibiotics. The doctor, who actually looked as cleancut and grandfatherly as Marcus Welby, said that I would be almost totally deaf in that ear for quite some time, but in three to six months my hearing would be normal again.

"After about a year, I mentioned to my mother that I still heard nothing with my left ear. But by then she was entirely immersed in her 'ways to alternative being,' which included daily prayer at a shrine made of sticks and stones and feathers she had built in the middle of our dining room, honoring the 'wild woman' in her. She told me that somehow I had 'created' my lack of hearing, that somehow it served me, and that it was important for me to appreciate my inventiveness. She assured me that when I no longer wanted, or needed, to be deaf, I would 'create' my hearing again. And since then I guess I have always believed that I am not really deaf."

Marie coughed and Marco looked up from his magazine.

"I was just thinking," he said, rather excitedly for a man who had just apparently been reading *Textile World*, "about the connection between Viagra and entangled particles. You know how, when observed, entangled particles will sometimes collapse into opposite states? It came to me that the worst sexual problem for a man is flaccidity and the worst sexual problem for a woman is frigidity. He softens and she hardens. The parallel is extraordinary."

As Marie sat in Maud Blake's kitchen, sipping vodka, she remembered how sorry she had been that day for having told Marco that story, which probably wasn't even true. She should have been working on her quantum paper instead of listening to the small lunatic expound on every preposterous thought that crept through his mind. She couldn't recall how she had responded to that particular inanity about men and women having complementary sexual ailments. If Marco was teaching her one thing, however, it was a new appreciation for autocensorship. Feeling slightly uneasy under the gaze of the orange cat with a superiority complex, she asked herself why she told this man, who was obviously missing some marbles, stories about her childhood. What was it about *her,* she wanted to know, that had caused her to select him, *of all people,* as her listener? And then it struck her that Rex had been saying the same thing to her that morning on the phone. He had been telling her that he was horrified to have chosen her, Marie, to tell his intimate story to, not so much because of what she might do with the story professionally but because he felt about her exactly the way she felt about Marco—Marie was never in a million years the person he imagined telling his stories to, true or false. What Rex had been calling to tell her that morning was that she was the wrong audience, the wrong woman.

"It was St. Vincent's." Marie hadn't heard Maud come back into the room, and she jumped. "I'm not sure if it's good news or bad news but she's come out of the coma. They say I should come to the hospital."

"I'm sorry," Marie said, unsure what exactly she was sorry for. Was she sorry that Nora Mars had come out of the coma—that she might live—and Marie wouldn't get to write her obituary? Was she sorry for Maud, who had to go see her deathly ill sister in the hospital after all this time? Was she sorry in anticipation of Nora Mars' death, or was she sorry she had been anticipating it?

"Can I give you a ride to the city?" she asked Maud. She simply had to assume that the actress was going to die, and two hours with Nora Mars' sister trapped in the seat next to hers would give Marie a perfect opportunity to seal up an exclusive. How was that for bloodthirsty?

Maud raised the eyebrow, then said, "Sure, but the interview is over. Give me a minute to get my bag. It's already packed."

Marie said, "One last question. What happened to your child?"

"I don't know," Maud said, her cold green eyes softening almost imperceptibly. "I never saw him. The doctor arranged everything." She left the room and Marie turned off the tape recorder and put it in her bag.

The day had warmed up quite a bit. Marie and Maud got into the Impala and glided, in silence, up Sycamore Lane toward Hopewell's Main Street. As they passed the fire station, the string of shops, the Congregational church, Marie thought enviously of Nora Mars. A pretty girl from a small town who wasn't afraid of thinking big, who somehow knew early on that life was about skidding along the edge of a precipice at high speed. She wondered what would have happened if Maud had gone to New York instead of Nora. Might her idol Nora Mars have never existed? Marie liked to imagine herself as someone who took risks, but in the end she inevitably chose to play it safe. Ironically, she thought to herself while suppressing a smirk, she lived her life as if she had something to lose.

Maud continued to say very little as Marie sped along the small country roads that led back to the Taconic Parkway. No matter what story she ended up writing, Marie thought, it was going to be a good one. She looked at her watch. After dropping Maud off at her hotel, she would go straight to the office and put together a draft. There was so much more she would like to know, but if Nora Mars died Marie had to be ready with something; otherwise Brewster would kill her. And if Nora held on, tomorrow morning, first thing, Marie would call Rex Mars—play the jealousy card—and get his reaction to Maud's version of things.

As they drove past some black-and-white cows grazing in a field, Maud said, "You've got balls driving to see me in this car. *The Reckoning* wasn't bad, but there were far better films made that year—*North by Northwest, Anatomy of a Murder, Compulsion.* Shall we put down the roof?"

Marie didn't know if she had just been complimented or slammed. She pulled the car over to the side of the road, unfastened the roof catches, and pushed the big square red button that said *Roof.* The top of the car cracked open like an oyster shell, rose upward, then folded itself away somewhere behind them. The warm spring air slid across Marie's skin and through her hair, and she decided she would keep the car through the weekend.

5

{ M O N E Y }

"Money rules all."
—CYRUS THE SLAVE

"You'd be surprised how much it cost to look this cheap."
—DOLLY PARTON

"Most of the universe is influenced by an abundance of some weird form of energy whose force is repulsive."
—MICHAEL S. TURNER

On Saturday afternoon Marie was, of course, early to meet Rex Mars and had forty-five minutes to kill. She was even earlier than usual due to the Impala, which now sat out amidst the other cars on the street like a diamond in a bed of gravel, a peacock in a murder of crows. She had finally reached Rex the night before and they had decided to meet at his apartment the next afternoon at three in a section of Brooklyn known as

DUMBO, a ridiculous acronym for "down under the Manhattan Bridge overpass." She had chosen to wait in a dingy pizzeria because there was nowhere else to go in the immediate neighborhood. A bodega was on one corner and a mechanic's shop was down the block. Otherwise the street was occupied by warehouses, both abandoned and not, although they all looked run-down. She wasn't hungry but ordered a slice and a Coke anyway so the guy behind the counter wouldn't get curious.

Friday evening, after dropping Maud off at her hotel, Marie had gone directly to the *Star*. She batted out onto the computer a version of the Rex Mars story, a version of the Maud Blake story, then tried to combine the two in a *he said/she said* piece that had potential. She put in a call to Rex Mars saying she wanted to get together with him at his earliest possible convenience. And she checked repeatedly with St. Vincent's Hospital: Nora Mars was still in the intensive-care unit but her condition had stabilized—whatever that meant—for the time being.

Just before midnight, as Marie was getting ready to go home, Brewster sauntered over to her cubicle. He looked fresh as a daisy in his yellow oxford shirt and his green-and-white-striped bow tie. One of Brewster's characteristics as boss was that he kept no regular hours. Sometimes he would be in the office for days at a stretch, then hardly at all for a week. He would come in at six one morning and leave at lunchtime, or he would arrive at six in the evening and not leave until the staff began arriving the next morning. Marie believed he kept these odd hours purely to keep his staff guessing as to his where-abouts, to keep himself very much on their minds.

"Nora Mars dead yet?" he asked, smiling.

"As if you wouldn't know," Marie answered.

"Bad luck all around if she pulls through, huh?" He winked.

Brewster and his betting buddy the sports editor, Dick Pen-rose, probably had some sort of office pool going on Nora Mars' day and hour of death. Brewster loved gambling; horses, box-ing, poker. He was up for any kind of bet. And though he was not particularly keen on science subjects, she remembered when he had Ned Brilliant do a long feature about Stephen Hawking's much publicized bet with fellow physicist Kip Thorne over whether a certain type of black hole called a naked singularity existed. Thorne eventually won a subscrip-tion to *Penthouse* magazine from Hawking, who claimed that a reality that allowed for such black holes was obscene (PENT-HOUSE MAGAZINE PROVES "OBSCENE" BLACK HOLES EXIST).

While doing the research for the piece, Marie had learned that betting among scientists was something of an epidemic. Hawking placed so many bets he needed a bookie to keep track of them all. Nobelist William Phillips bet one hundred dollars plus interest that no unexplained surprises would turn up in the physics of the quantum microworld anytime over the next fifty years. Physicist James Peebles was referee for an international bet on the value of the Hubble constant, a number that describes the rate of expansion of the universe. And both Bell

Labs and SLAC had notebooks recording regular running bets on things like competing explanations for superconductivity and the existence and mass of the top quark.

Marie also learned that the scientific wager was by no means a new phenomenon: In 1600 Johannes Kepler bet Tycho Brahe's assistant Longomontanus that he would figure out the problem of Mars' orbit around the sun in a week; he lost the bet but came up with the solution five years later. Isaac Newton's *Principia* grew out of the paper he wrote competing for a prize offered by Christopher Wren, the English architect and scientist. And the physicist Richard Feynman gave 50-to-1 odds on a dollar bet and paid off when experiments in 1957 showed that the laws of physics were not quite symmetrical when reversed, as in a mirror. Brewster called Ned's article "superb" and Ned had, as usual, taken all the credit.

"For a while there this afternoon the odds didn't look too great for our Nora," Brewster said, still winking. "But she's tough as nails. I bet she holds on a lot longer than expected. Your cell phone was off today. Why?"

It was at times like this that Marie thought of Brewster as Santa Claus. He knows when you are sleeping. He knows when you're awake. Marie often forgot to turn her cell phone on. Brewster had yelled at her before about it. She'd turned it off when she went into Maud Blake's house and had neglected to turn it back on when they got in the car.

"I had Nora Mars' sister in the car with me. I didn't want us to be interrupted."

"I see," Brewster said in a tone that said, I don't see at all.

"She's never talked to the press about her sister. She talked to me."

"Good work. Any idea what she wants?" Brewster asked.

Marie remembered Maud's parting words to her a few hours earlier: "You be careful now," she had said before disappearing into the lobby of the Excelsior Hotel on West Eighty-first Street. Marie had no idea what she was referring to—her driving?—but she heard in Maud's words a warning, one of those big life warnings. But what was it? Be careful of Rex Mars? Be careful of what you write? Be careful of becoming a bitter old maid like her? Be careful of being careful?

They had said very little to each other during the drive from Hopewell to Manhattan. It had been literally impossible to hear until Marie pulled off the road just before the exit for the Cross Bronx Expressway and put up the roof. In the distance was an elevated subway station with people scattered about the brightly lit platform. In the shadows, Marie saw a man and a woman kissing. It reminded her of Celia Johnson and Trevor Howard in *Brief Encounter*. She pulled back onto the highway, told herself now or never, and said to Maud, "There's something I need to discuss with you."

Without taking a breath, Maud said, "I know. You want an exclusive and you'll talk to your boss to see how much money or vouchers or perks or stocks or whatever imitates money you can get to keep me loyal."

Marie felt an overwhelming sense of relief. Maud had just made it abundantly clear that other journalists had already been here, already made the offer. In fact, the wording of her statement had the distinct feel of Ned Brilliant at the *Post*. And yet Maud, at least for the moment, was in Marie's car, not in Ned's (a Mercedes) or anyone else's. Marie turned onto the West Side Highway and watched in the rearview mirror as the George Washington Bridge receded behind them. She was just a little ahead of the game.

"This isn't about money, though, Marie," Maud continued.

Marie was immediately suspicious. She thought, Isn't everything about money? Wasn't Marx at least right about that?

"Nora's made so much of it, I've lost my taste for it," Maud explained.

Marie recalled what Nora Mars had said when she founded her investment company: "Whoever says that money can't buy you happiness doesn't know where to shop."

"Why do you think Nora gave up her acting career?" Marie asked.

Maud looked at her with an eyebrow raised. Although her expression was still full of condescension, this time, Marie was convinced, it was mingled with pity. "We all grow old," she said, then added, "Nora knew her days were numbered in Hollywood and she had a lot of ex-husbands to support—not to mention me. Money was one of the few things Nora truly trusted."

Marie speculated on how much money Rex had received from Nora Mars in his divorce settlement. Marie figured it was not a huge sum, maybe a few hundred thousand, which he had undoubtedly run through by now. He probably had a trickle of an income from his music and had made a nice chunk of change on his advance for his memoir. He might just have enough left of that, she mused, to buy her a modest diamond from Tiffany's when the time came.

("I don't care where his heart is, only his money." Nora Mars, *Two Deaths*, 1966.)

"If I decide to talk to you," Maud went on, "and only to you about my sister's life, about my life, I want something for it, but not money."

"What, then?" Marie asked, wary of such devotion from Maud.

"Excitement, engagement, a little flicker of eternity."

"But how can *I* give you that?" Marie asked.

"You can't. Nora once said, 'The poor wish to be rich, the rich wish to be happy, the single wish to be married, and the married wish to be dead.' "

Marie knew—and loved—the quote. Nora had said it on the steps of City Hall after filing for her fifth divorce.

Marie pulled the Impala up in front of the Excelsior Hotel. "I don't understand," she said.

Maud got out of the car. "I'm glad to be wishing for something, Marie, and I'm glad I met you." And then she had added, "You be careful now," before disappearing into the hotel lobby.

Marie stared at Brewster, who was riffling through the papers on her desk. "I have no idea what Maud Blake wants but you'll be relieved to know that it's not money," Marie said.

"Well, as my father always said, beware of the things money can't buy." Brewster walked off with drafts of a couple of stories Marie was working on, but not the Nora Mars obituary, which she had carefully concealed. She couldn't stand his habit of reading pieces in their earliest form, but Brewster said it kept his writers' egos in check. "Tomorrow," he called from his office door, "do me a favor and leave your cell phone on." When Marie finally left the *Star* well after midnight, she had a draft that would impress even Santa Claus.

Saturday morning Marie had woken up early. At first she was reluctant to get out of bed and give up her dreams, which had been full of Rex Mars. But then she realized she was going to need a while to find just the right outfit for their meeting. After several cups of instant coffee and an inordinate amount of time spent in front of her mirror experimenting with every possible combination her wardrobe offered, she put together the perfect combo: dark gray slacks, a mildly transparent blue linen blouse (she had agonized over whether to wear linen in March but the temperatures *were* in the seventies and rising), her most ornate black bra, and black boots with a half-inch heel. She had to admit, the overall effect was enticingly demure.

("I dress for women, I undress for men." Nora Mars, *Dark Blue*, 1965.)

She then called Maud Blake at the Excelsior and left her cell phone number on the voice mail even though Maud already had it. She called St. Vincent's and was given a similar spiel as the night before about Nora Mars' condition—critical but stable. She was ready for Rex Mars. She calculated that it would take her at the very most an hour in the Impala to get to DUMBO from Chelsea. Since she had four hours to get there, and the heat wave made the day smell of June, on a whim she decided to take a detour to Coney Island.

Walking to the nearby garage where she had parked the car overnight, she felt shivers of pleasure at the thought of soon being enveloped by all that glamour. Marie, who had taken most of the stringer dumps from Milan during the Gucci murder trial, was beginning to empathize with Patricia Gucci's self-professed passion for the finer things of life—including cars. While on the stand being questioned by prosecutors about her role in her famous fashion designer husband's death, she was accused of having an excessive need to spend money. "Let's just put it this way," the widow declared. "I would rather weep in a Rolls-Royce than be happy on a bicycle."

Top down, the convertible breezed over the Brooklyn Bridge, out the BQE to Coney Island. Sunglasses on, hair windswept, mood sky-high, Marie was Vittorio Gassman in *The Overtake*, Sophia Loren in *Arabesque*, Nora Mars in *The Reckoning*. She took a stroll on the boardwalk, ate a foot-long hot dog from Nathan's, and played a few games of Skee-Ball, imagining a future in which she did all these things with Rex. She attempted to buy a set of hexagonal blue glass jars for her kitchen from a junk shop owned by a nasty old Russian woman. When Marie tried to bargain for them, the woman took immediate offense and refused to sell Marie the jars even for the originally stated price of ten dollars. Marie would have left the shop then and there but she wanted the jars. They were a strange cloudy blue, and their shapes were so peculiar the jars were virtually useless. The tall one was too tall and thin, the middle one too squat, and the small one was so small that at best it might hold a few tooth-picks. Only after the woman's two cronies yelled at her for several minutes in Russian did she relent and take Marie's ten-dollar bill. Marie had no idea why she bought jars for a kitchen she barely even entered. But she didn't care. Desired and got, she thought, feeling pleased as punch.

Although it was not something she would readily admit to, Marie adored money. She adored earning it, having it, wanting it, buying things with it, winning it, and even losing it, which had happened on a few occasions with Ned Brilliant during weekends in Atlantic City. She found money to be extremely compelling. But at the same time she was embarrassed by it. She didn't like to talk about it or ask for it. She didn't want to understand it or her relationship to it. So the other day, when Marco had brought the subject up at the library, she was initially very annoyed.

Deciding to take a break from her quantum paper, she grabbed a magazine and sat down next to Marco, who was reading the *Federal Reserve Bulletin*. "Did you know," he said, straightening up in his chair, "that Bill Gates makes so much money an hour that if he saw a five-hundred-dollar bill lying on the floor it wouldn't be worth his time to pick it up?"

"I wonder what it would be like to have that much money," Marie said, settling down into her chair.

"You're missing the point," Marco said. "Today, money is information. It has become almost exclusively a virtual commodity. Money's reality is as a piece of paper that promises to pay you more pieces of paper. It has no real worth, only virtual worth. We run around hoarding it, desiring it, spending it, wasting it, ignoring it, hating it, seeing it as the cause of all evil, the route to all happiness. Money is not simply a symbolic barter system for material goods or even for information; it is a force."

"Whatever," Marie said, waving her hand dismissively. "I just want enough to buy myself a big fat diamond ring when I turn forty."

Marco went on as if he hadn't heard her. "Have you ever noticed the parallel between money and the cosmological constant?"

"No," Marie said, thinking she was a hopeless glutton for Marco-style punishment.

"I just read," Marco said, "that the cosmological constant is a theoretical antigravity force, an energy from the vacuum of space that attenuates the effects of mass gravity and keeps the universe in a state of equilibrium. The universe is, in theory, permeated by this repulsive force, the opposite of gravity, which is responsible for keeping the universe from either collapsing of its own weight or expanding into vanishing infinity. Money functions as a similar force for the human race. It affects and connects every last one of us and maintains among us a certain equilibrium. Some of the most transcendent minds—Ralph Waldo Emerson, Andy Warhol, and, of course, Milton Friedman—were all very aware of the money force."

"Emerson?" Marie asked in spite of herself.

"Yes. Ralph said, 'Money, which represents the prose of life, and which is hardly spoken of in parlors without an apology, is, in its effects and laws, as beautiful as roses.' Andy revived the crucial link between art and commerce, declaring 'making money is art, and working is art, and good business is the best art of all,' and Milton summed up the law of conservation of money with his observation. 'There's no such thing as a free lunch.' The money force ensures a zero-sum game—there is no profit without another's loss. But by the same token, so to speak, the losers must have something to lose in order for the winners to win."

"Sounds like a wacky argument for capitalism to me," Marie said, feeling exhausted by Marco's freewheeling brain. She contemplated his possible money situation. He certainly wasn't making a dime as a freelance intellectual, although he was evidently putting his time in. He didn't appear to have any kind of regular job. She decided he was independently wealthy, which still made him suspicious but was nevertheless an improvement over her previous supposition that he was a homeless escapee from an insane asylum.

"Capitalism and communism—these are just large systemized expressions of the profound embarrassment that accompanies money."

"Embarrassment?" Marie sat up.

"One of the definitions of embarrassment is, in fact, 'to cause financial difficulties to.' Our interaction with money inevitably makes us self-conscious—a state we will do anything to overcome. So we have too little money, we want more: embarrassment fuels progress. We have too much money, we want to give it away: embarrassment fuels philanthropy. We have no money and no way of ever getting any, so we hope for it in the next life: embarrassment fuels religion. And so on. As a species we have a repugnance for embarrassment and yet it is a fundamental force of human nature that is key to our equilibrium, our survival."

"That's interesting," Marie said flatly, but then, unable to control herself, she pointed out to Marco that the cosmological constant—also known as x-matter or quintessence—was a force originally proposed by Einstein, and later considered by him to be the biggest embarrassment of his career. He completely abandoned the idea. "Now its prediction might well turn out to be one of his greatest triumphs," Marie sighed. She had long found embarrassment to be an accurate Geiger counter for truth. At the same time, however, embarrassment worked extremely hard to discourage even the most brilliant and courageous from discovering that truth.

Making her way back to the Impala, which she had parked in front of the dilapidated roller coaster across from Nathan's, she suddenly had the paranoid thought that the Russian women had staged the whole scene in order to get her to pay far too high a price for the blue bottles. They were probably a freebie that came with a full gas tank or could be had for a few Skee-Ball tickets. She decided it didn't matter what the truth was, because she loved the bottles. She placed them, wrapped in Cyrillic newspaper, carefully on the passenger seat. As she floated in the Impala along the Shore Parkway on her way to meet Rex, she felt as if she were sailing rather than driving. She used her cell phone to check her messages both at work and at home. None from Maud, none from Brewster. She called St. Vincent's. Nora Mars was still alive.

It took her only fifteen minutes to arrive in DUMBO, that deserted area of Brooklyn named after a humiliated baby elephant, where she was presently eating pizza and drinking Coke while trying to analyze why her calculations were so consistently off the mark. She soon moved on to her customary litany of self-loathing, but somewhere around the part about how useless, even detrimental, she felt her job was to the betterment of mankind—and how she wasn't ever going to get married, much less have children—she stopped and indulged in what she now privately referred to as a "Marcothought."

She suddenly saw herself as the embodiment of an advanced wave from John Wheeler and Richard Feynman's advanced wave theory. When energy or light is emitted, there are always two waves launched. The advanced wave travels backward in time; the other wave, the retarded wave, is the one we perceive. According to these physicists' description of light, we could theoretically see a light wave before it was even sent. The advanced wave *anticipates* what is to come. Effect precedes cause. Hadn't Marco pointed out that by being chronically early she was anticipating the other's absence? Her fear of being abandoned—and by this she guessed Marco was referring to her father leaving, but it could be her mother leaving or even Michael leaving—made her anticipate events from the past in the present. And because she was anticipating an event in the past that would never happen in the present, did that mean she was somehow changing—correcting—the past?

Or was she simply incessantly repeating the past in the present? Of course, all of this speculation was moot as it was impossible, due to entropy, to extract any information from the advanced waves. And, in any case, all the equations of physics from Einstein onward say that time as we perceive it doesn't actually exist.

"I hope you don't mind." A thirtyish woman with short blond corkscrew curls was pointing at a small, white-haired poodle with a rhinestone-studded collar standing at her feet. Marie gave the woman a confused, guilty look, as if she had been caught babbling Marcothink in public and was being asked to kindly refrain.

"Some people get disgusted," the woman explained over the din of the subway crossing the Manhattan Bridge. "You know, eating in the same room with a dog. But he's very clean, aren't you, Tarzan?" She leaned down and gave the dog a bite of her pizza.

"Not at all," Marie said, utterly disgusted, but grateful to the woman for having interrupted her rambling thoughts. The dog now had a little red beard from the tomato sauce.

"Tarzan loves pizza, and not just any pizza," she said, sitting down at the next table, licking her fingers. "You know, this place has the best pizza in Brooklyn. But don't tell anyone or it will be over. Look what happened to Ray's. He may have single-handedly destroyed the whole concept of original. Have you been here before?"

"No," Marie said with measured bluntness. She had a newspaper open in front of her and began intently reading an article about the serious health problems caused by religious ritual bathing in the heavily polluted waters of the Ganges. Throughout her twenties, Marie had humored anyone who struck up a conversation with her. She felt it would be rude to show her lack of interest and she had believed in the credo "You never know who you might meet." With age and wisdom, however, she had learned that the overwhelming probability was that most people who struck up random conversations with you were boring oddballs who had lost all touch with reality, had nothing else to do with their time—and thought you didn't either. For years, Marie wondered if these encounters only happened to her, if these weirdos saw something in her that they recognized and singled her out for a chat between comrades. She had long since learned how to nip these conversations in the bud, cut these interminable yakety-yaks off at the pass. At the ripe age of thirty-nine, Marie was a pro. But then she remembered Marco Trentadue, the Great Exception. As hard as she tried, she couldn't figure out what it was about him that caused her to disregard years of painfully collected empirical evidence and engage.

("The more I get to know other people, the better I like myself." Nora Mars, *The Diva*, 1977.)

The guy behind the pizza counter was almost yelling. "You're twenty-nine cents short," he said, pointing to a pile of change in front of a man wearing an old stained overcoat and wheeling a baby carriage full of empty bottles and cans.

"I ain't got it."

"No money, no slice."

"Ah, man, let me slide."

"No way," said the stocky, mustached man behind the counter as he grabbed back the slice of pizza and pushed the guy's pile of change back toward him.

"I'm hungry."

"Too bad."

It was hot outside, hot inside. Both men were sweating.

"You gonna make me beg for it?"

"You already are begging."

Marie remembered begging Brewster to let her do the Nora Mars story, and she remembered Rex begging her not to write about Nora Mars' dead baby. Maybe Nora was well on her way to recovery and it had all been for nothing. Another train rumbled by over their heads.

"Twenty-nine cents," the man yelled. He wore no shoes. His feet were wrapped in cloth and plastic and tied up with twine. "Will anyone give me twenty-nine cents so I can eat a piece of pizza?" Marie and the woman with the poodle were the only customers. The man shuffled over to where they were sitting.

"You got twenty-nine cents?" he asked Tarzan's owner. Marie was relieved he wasn't asking her.

"I got it," said the blonde, picking up her dog. "But I'm not giving it to you. Get a life."

"Ah, man," he said, shaking his head, "that's harsh. All I want is twenty-nine cents. No strings attached." He was now standing in front of Marie. She was still pretending to read the article about the Ganges. She noticed out of the corner of her eye that her knapsack was sitting open on the table next to her. Her wallet was easily visible, easily accessible. She felt a trickle of sweat roll down her back.

"Please, miss," he said, "the pizza is gonna get cold."

Marie looked up. Her eyes locked with his—black flecked with gold like her own. He had a crescent-shaped scar that went from the corner of his eye to the middle of his chin. He was probably her age. She thought of her brother, Michael, and their Third Grand (insoluble) Enigma: *Does the world obey a law, or is it only a chaos in which forces clash at random?*

She gave the guy a dollar, inviting the intense scowls of the poodle woman and the pizza man. She knew that there had been an equal, or greater, probability of her telling the homeless guy, as she had so many others, "Sorry, not today." She looked at her watch. She was eight minutes late for Rex.

Rex's building was a five-story warehouse that had evidently been converted into five lofts. The names next to the buzzers—Wu, Applebaum, Johannson, Perez, and Mars (she pressed the button)—indicated private residences. The entranceway was tiny and the floor was littered with takeout menus. Marie could see an elevator, standard industrial self-operated, just inside the inner door. Finding her reflection in the glass door, she dabbed on red lipstick and pushed her hair behind her ears. Clara Bow.

As she was waiting for Rex to buzz her in, she tried to predict whether anything would happen between them, and, if it did, whether it was going to be something that would last. Although her knowledge of quantum mechanics told her that absolute physical laws were obsolete and the scientific world was now viewed only in terms of beautifully precise probabilities, she had always secretly sided with the hidden-variable theorists, who believed that—whether we can know it or not—everything in the universe has a predetermined destiny. She could see how quantum mechanics, with its time travel, its many-world realities, even its infinities, could have a romantic appeal to certain nonlinear sci-fi-prone minds—like Michael's or Marco's. But as far as she was concerned, fate was the sexiest word in the English language.

She buzzed again.

She wondered if she and Rex Mars were fated to be together, if it was written somewhere, encoded somehow in their DNA—or better yet in the universe's equivalent of DNA, the cosmic background radiation, the pervasive echo from the Big Bang where tiny temperature variations held the secrets of cosmic destiny. It was 3:17. Marie pressed the buzzer again. Perhaps he had gone out to get a bite to eat, milk, a bottle of whiskey, and was late getting back. Rex struck her as the late type although he had been at the Ear Inn before she was. Someday she would ask him why. She buzzed again.

What if he stood her up? She decided it wouldn't be a problem. He would be standing up a tabloid journalist, not her—there was nothing personal here yet. She buzzed one more time. She'd wait until 3:30 and then go. She already had a good story and her crush on Rex Mars was dangerous, not to mention self-destructive. Professionally, she could screw herself if it ever became known they had screwed (there she went again acting as an advanced wave), and personally, Rex Mars did not exactly fit her fantasy of the ideal husband. As Maud Blake so acutely pointed out, Rex Mars was a problem-riddled abandoned child in search of a mother, not a mature man in search of a lifelong soulmate.

Marie heard a buzzing noise and jumped to push open the door as if it might be her only chance to get inside. As she rode the elevator to the fifth floor, she threw caution to the wind, reminding herself that *all* men were looking for a mother and that it would be entirely unfair of her to hold that against Rex.

The elevator doors opened into a roller-rink-size loft. At the far end a wall of windows looked out over the East River, with the Manhattan Bridge, the Brooklyn Bridge, and Wall Street laid out before her like the backdrop for a musical. A good New Yorker, she immediately wanted to know how much he paid in rent. The elevator doors closed behind her as she stepped inside. Rex was nowhere in sight.

6

{ SCIENCE }

*"The whole of science is nothing more than
a refinement of everyday thinking."*
—ALBERT EINSTEIN

"It is the task of science to reduce deep truths to trivialities."
—NIELS BOHR

*"There ain't no answer. There ain't going to be any answer.
There never has been an answer. That's the answer."*
—GERTRUDE STEIN

Rex Mars appeared from behind a curtain like the wizard in *The Wizard of Oz*. "I'm sorry, I must have dozed off. Good thing you were persistent. I was dreaming I was being attacked by a dentist's drill. Finally, I realized it was only the buzzer," he explained, through a guilty grin. His hair was tousled, his eyes puffy, and he had obviously just woken from a serious sleep, not from any catnap. He was wearing the same getup he had worn to the Ear Inn: jeans, a snug white T-shirt, and his cobalt-blue alligator-skin cowboy boots. Marie wondered if he slept in them.

The apartment was not at all the bachelor pad she had been expecting—no mirrors on the ceiling, no king-size bed in the middle of the room. Still, it did have a certain seventies feel to it. First off, the curtains hiding the bed were made of blue-and-red bamboo beads hanging from pipes running along the ceiling. A picnic table painted black and covered with graffiti sat in front of the kitchen area, off to the right. At the far end of the loft, near the windows, a black velvet couch and two leather armchairs surrounded a glass coffee table. Against one wall was a curly-maple console and lumped beside it were two beanbag chairs, one bright orange, one magenta. A lawyer's bookcase flanked an architect's drawing table, which evidently served as a desk. Mostly what Marie saw, however, was empty space.

As she stood by the door taking in all that latitude, she thought how grand it would be to have such a large apartment, but then she envisioned herself in it with all her clutter and felt a little panicky. In the fifteen years she had been living in her small one-bedroom fifth-floor walk-up in a brownstone in Chelsea, she had never felt such fondness for her petite abode as she did in that moment. Perhaps, she thought, so much space wasn't good for Rex. He needed the spaces in his life to be filled; he needed someone to take care of him, someone who could understand him and help him find himself.

"C'mon in," Rex said, lightly pulling on her arm. "Come

look at the view. It'll make you green with envy, though I do have to live in a wasteland to get it."

The journey across the expansive loft was long, giving Marie time to despise the outfit she had chosen to wear. The pants kept riding up her boots; she had been sweating, so the shirt was sticking to her, and whoever wore linen in March, no matter how sweltering it was outside? When they finally arrived at the open windows, Marie hardly noticed the Lower Manhattan skyline, so intent was she on figuring out a way to get out of her clothes fast. Maybe then Rex wouldn't have time to notice her utter lack of taste. This thought led Marie to begin calculating that if Rex really were the Casanova she believed he was, seducing an average of three women a week over the past twenty years, she could be the three-thousand-one-hundred-and-twentieth woman to stand in that exact same position staring at that exact same stupendous cliché of a view.

A subway vibrated somewhere nearby. Marie took a deep breath. The air in the room had the faint and oddly pleasant smell of cigarettes and men's cologne. "Rex," she said, turning toward him, her voice full of sincerity, "I am very glad I met you. I even admit to feeling a rather strong attraction to you." Marie's directness was most astonishing to herself. She forced herself to look at Rex for his reaction, terrified of what she might find in his expression. Instead, he was beaming—wide smile, slight flush, sparkling eyes. "All the same," she continued, "I'm going to use at least some of what you told me in my article. I have a feeling, however, that you know the story about Nora Mars' dead baby isn't true."

His smile faded and his brow furrowed in what appeared to be confusion. "Isn't true?"

"I went to see Maud Blake."

He sat down heavily on the couch and took a neatly rolled joint from a large silver cigarette box with the initials *N.M.* elaborately engraved on the top. Placing the joint in the corner of his mouth, he picked up a lighter that matched the cigarette box, and lit up. He inhaled deeply and, holding the joint out for Marie to take, waited a good long while before he exhaled.

The last time Marie had gotten stoned she had been with her brother, Michael. It was the day before she was supposed to leave for graduate school and he had come over to say good-bye, or rather to sing it. As they smoked one joint and then another, he sang all the choruses to "So Long, Farewell" from *The Sound of Music.*

In the middle of their unstoppable belly laughs, Michael managed to articulate the following: "Marie, you're going to graduate school because you wish you were me."

Marie was laughing so hysterically she actually had the paranoid thought she might suffocate.

"Why you want to be me I'll never know," he went on, breathing heavily between giggles. "It must be a sibling thing. You wish you were good in science and math like I am and could be a cosmologist." More snickering, snorts.

"Do you remember," Marie said between gasps, "the first day of Mr. Waugh's class when he said, 'Science is like pornography. I can't define it but I know it when I see it'?" More

laughter. Then, trying to maintain a certain level of serious-
ness, Marie added, "Michael, you have nothing to do with my
going to graduate school. I'm going because I want to increase
my chances of finding a husband like Mr. Waugh. And besides,
I am going to study philosophy not science."

"In any case," Michael said, sobering up, "it comes down to
this: you're good at writing and you're bad at science and what
you like about science is what you love about writing—the details, the precision, the wish to get to the heart of the matter,
the metaphors, the unanswerable questions, the answers that
only ask more questions, the playfulness, the seduction. But the
really funny thing is," and he dissolved into uncontrollable
laughter, Marie joining him although she had no idea what was
so funny. "The really funny thing is," he repeated, finally getting ahold of himself, "that *I* should go to graduate school in
physics but won't because I want to be you." And then he sang
to her King Louie's song from *The Jungle Book*.

The next day Marie left for graduate school; ten months
later she had dropped out and was no longer on speaking terms
with Michael; fifteen years later she and her brother still
weren't speaking. But that was another story.

Marie walked over to where Rex was sitting on the couch
and took the joint from his outstretched hand, trying to pinch
it between her thumb and forefinger. For a few seconds their
hands were awkwardly entwined. She inhaled, handed it back,
was horrified to see she'd left a lipstick mark on it, exhaled.

"It's been a while," she said, smiling at Rex, although she

felt like bawling. The idea that she didn't speak to her brother was unfathomable to her. As kids, they had pricked their fingers and combined their blood, just in case there had been a mix-up in the hospital and they weren't biologically related. They had sworn that they would gladly die for each other, and they had a tacit understanding that the one thing both of them wanted more than anything was for their parents to get back together. Later on, they had even come to agree on the great mysteries of the universe, devising the Four Grand (insoluble) Enigmas.

There could be no doubt that Michael's silence was entirely Marie's fault. But how could two siblings, once so devoted to each other, become so estranged? She looked at Rex, who was toking away, and thought of Nora and Maud. She reflected on their relationship—Maud had to be livid that Nora had stolen the life that was meant to be hers. Marie sat down on the couch next to Rex. She reached over for the joint and he obliged.

"Did Nora and Maud get along?" she asked, inhaling while imagining the dramatic death of myriad brain cells.

("Die, die, go on, I want to see you die." Nora Mars, *Shadows of the Heart*, 1967.)

"They hated each other," Rex said, grinning. "The reason was something dumb like Nora stole Maud's high school sweetheart and Maud could never forgive her."

Marie's lungs felt as if they were being caressed with steel wool. She coughed and coughed until tears were rolling down her cheeks. Something dumb, she agreed, coughing. Rex patted her on the back and she put up a hand to tell him to stop, giving the joint back to him. This time she had been careful to hold it in such a way that her lipstick didn't get on it—instead she had big red marks on her fingers. She cringed at the thought of what her lipstick must look like. The inside of her mouth felt as if it had grown fur.

"I know just the remedy for cotton mouth," Rex said, standing, and in a strong, mellifluous tenor, he began to sing: *"Summertime and the livin' is easy, Fish are jumpin' and the cotton is fine, Oh your daddy's rich, and your mama's good lookin'…"*

Marie coughed lightly between giggles. She couldn't believe Rex was singing to her. She wondered just who was seducing whom in this scenario and to what purpose. She wanted a story and a husband, not necessarily in that order. What did Rex want?

"What was the title again of the dreadful musical Nora made?" she asked.

Rex was obviously impressed. The movie was rarely shown, an obscure relic known only to the most diligent archaeologists of Marsiana. *"Head Over Heels.* She was terrible, couldn't sing or dance. By comparison, she made Joan Crawford look sublime in *Dancing Lady.* Nora insisted the studio retrieve and bury all prints." Rex let the joint smolder in the silver ashtray also engraved with Nora's initials. "Here's another good one for us." And again, loud and lovely: *"We're having a heat wave, a tropical heat wave, The temp'rature's rising, it isn't surprising…,"* which melded into *"It's too darn hot, it's too darn hot.*

I'd like to sup with my baby tonight, Refill the cup with my baby tonight, But I ain't up to my baby tonight, . . . 'Cause it's too darn hot . . ." He then skipped across the loft to the door, where he grabbed a big black umbrella from an umbrella stand, opened it, and twirled around the huge floor joyously crooning, *"I'm singin' in the rain, Just singin' in the rain, What a glorious feeling, I'm happy again, I'm laughing at clouds, So dark up above, The sun's in my heart, And I'm ready for love . . ."* In the middle of his performance, the umbrella collapsed over his head and Marie, in her stoned state, thought it was the funniest thing she had ever seen in her life. She fell back on the couch laughing, pounding her fists into the cushions. When she realized that her levity was perhaps out of proportion, she tried to control herself by clenching her teeth together. This seemed to work, although once again tears began pouring from her eyes. Rex, who had reopened the umbrella and continued to leap around his loft, was now singing, *"They all laughed at Christopher Columbus, When he said the world was round, They all laughed when Edison recorded sound, They all laughed at Wilbur and his brother, When they said that man could fly . . ."*

When he had finished his performance, Marie clapped, Rex bowed, then plopped down on the couch next to her, holding the umbrella over them. His brow was speckled with small silvery beads of sweat which Marie was tempted to wipe away. She knew if she touched him it was all over and that's what he was waiting for. She had to choose: Rex Mars or the story.

She put her hand to her throat and said, "I'm so thirsty.

Could I have a glass of water?" Maybe if she stalled, she'd figure out a way to have both.

Rex let go of the umbrella, which toppled behind the couch. He stood up. "An unfortunate side effect," he said, his words sticky. He went to the refrigerator and brought back two glasses and a bottle of Evian.

Marie drank and then was overcome by a desire to sleep. Her eyelids felt like tiny lead curtains. The intensity of everything—Rex, the singing, the colored beanbags, the orange-tinted overheated Manhattan out the window, the blue boots—made Marie very tired. She decided to close her eyes just for a minute in order to give herself a chance to get it back together, regroup, relax. As she lay back on the black velvet couch, she thought of Marco and how when she was with him she sometimes had the sensation that she was on drugs. She remembered that he, too, had sung to her on a balmy evening not long ago at the library.

"In some parallel universe, the job of a particle physicist is as lyricist for a never-ending musical epic entitled *The Tower of Babel.*" Marco was expounding on a new theory of his. "They study the subatomic world in order to provide new words for the songs in the musical."

Marie rested her head on the back of the chair feeling a little giddy for no good reason. "Don't you have anything better to do?" she asked.

"I have evidence."

"Evidence, schmevidence. Scientists spend hundreds of

years compiling evidence that ultimately proves the unreliability of that evidence."

Then to the tune of "Do-Re-Mi," Marco began to sing:

Quark, a bit, a charming whit
Muon, a lepton that says no
Mie, a scattering of myself
Spin, a schizoid place to go
String, a theory way ahead
Loops, have yet to make a show
M, the math fills God with dread
That will bring us back to Squark

Marie was reviewing in her head everything she had eaten and drunk that day that might have been somehow tampered with. The only explanation for what she was perceiving to be happening in the library was that she had been drugged.

"And that's not all," Marco continued. "There are actually practitioners of the particle lyricist movement in our present universe. For example, the Cernettes."

"The Cernettes?"

"An all-female all-particle-physicist rock group. By day, the four band members work for CERN, the high-energy particle laboratory in Geneva, and they croon by night. Their songs include the hits 'Antiworld,' 'Microwave Love,' and 'Strong Interaction,' which goes," and again Marco broke into song, *"You quark me up, you quark me down, you quark me top, you quark me bottom."*

"Sounds obscene," Marie said, checking her pulse and her ability to focus.

"And then there's Dr. Juan Maldacena and Dr. Jeffrey Harvey, who hip-hop about M-theory and p-branes. And the most popular of all is Dr. Lynda Williams, a physicist and former go-go dancer who gyrates to songs about supersymmetry."

"Your point?"

He hesitated before answering. "You," he said. "I've been trying to understand your thing for science. I mean, it just seems so unlike you to be fascinated by people who measure rigid rods in spacetime. Besides, aren't you a little suspicious of a discipline in which the physical world is discussed in terms of measuring the lengths of hard, sticklike objects?"

Marie laughed. "You've got me all wrong. I didn't go to graduate school to study physics or astronomy," she explained, "but the philosophical implications of those sciences, so I wasn't doing any measuring myself." Marie leaned back in her chair. "But you've got a point. Because Einstein liked to measure big things, and Bohr liked to measure little things, their ideas about reality were vastly different."

"Petals pulled from the same flower," Marco said, flipping through the pages of *Horticulture Monthly*. "She loves me, she loves me not."

"Clarify," Marie said, frustrated she was yet again being forced to ask for an explanation she could do without.

"Cosmic complementarity. There is a theory of everything that explains all phenomena in spacetime; there is not a theory of everything that explains all phenomena in spacetime."

"You mean, say, a theory of everything versus Gödel's incompleteness theorem?" Marie asked, deciding that she really had to stop encouraging these conversations with Marco.

"Not 'versus,' *and*. Both are possible, probable. She can love you and not love you simultaneously. Petals from the same flower."

Marie sighed. She thought of taking drugs the next time she met up with Marco to see if he might seem more normal to her.

"Why did you quit graduate school?" he asked, glancing at his watch, perusing his magazine.

"I don't know," Marie answered, staring at the ceiling. "I just had this overwhelming feeling that I wasn't supposed to be doing that, there, then. I felt I was supposed to be doing something else with my life, although I'm not sure it was tabloid journalism." Lowering her voice, she added, "And it may—although I emphasize 'may'—have had something to do with measuring: with not measuring up."

Marco put down *Horticulture Monthly* and selected a copy of *In These Times* from his stack of newspapers and magazines. He smiled, then sighed. "Well, well. I can hardly blame you. Our world's phallologocentrism is so oppressive to women."

Marie sat up abruptly. "If there is one thing I can't stand, it's a man who claims to be a feminist. It's an oxymoron. I quit graduate school because I quit. Not because I'm a woman and couldn't hack it. I quit because I was tired of being in my head all the time. I found it boring and limiting. I wanted to be more at the center of things, in the city, interacting, thinking about *real* people's *real* problems every day."

"Liberal drivel," Marco said. "You do realize, of course," he went on, "that there is no such thing as the center of things. Copernicus, Galileo, Newton, Darwin, Einstein, Hubble, and Heisenberg have all contributed to that conclusion. We're not at the center of our solar system; we're in a remote spiral arm of our galaxy. Even our universe may be some tiny fluctuation in an infinity of universes. We're not the center of anything. The very idea is scientifically disallowed."

Marie wasn't listening to Marco's little diatribe. Instead, she was asking herself why exactly she came to the library, why she continued to work obsessively on a paper she had begun for her first-year second-semester seminar in the philosophy of physics. The seminar had ended, the semester had ended, her relationship with Michael had ended, and still she hadn't finished the paper. In the fall she did not go back to school but got a job as a fact-checker (another oxymoron) at the *Gotham City Star*. After a few years, she was promoted to junior reporter, which meant the same job only now and again Brewster sent her out on a story no one else wanted to do. And still she continued to work diligently on the philosophy of science paper for her graduate school seminar. At first, she had believed that if she could just finish it, things would come together for her professionally and personally. But after a while, what she believed the finished paper might cause to happen in the future became irrelevant. Working on the paper itself was now a compulsion that she could no longer imagine her life without.

An early evening breeze came off the East River and Marie

shivered. "Rex," she said, throwing off sleep and sitting up on the black velvet couch. "Are you happy?"

"Of course I'm happy," he said, opening his eyes. He was slumped in one of the leather armchairs. "It takes imagination to be unhappy." He paused, drank some water, lit a cigarette.

She leaned back on the couch. Rex was quoting someone, maybe Nora, but Marie couldn't place it. One thing she did know, though, was that she was going to be terribly disappointed when she left DUMBO without having had sex with Rex Mars. But she had a job to do. She drank three glasses of water in succession, then said, "Maud told me Nora never gave birth to, much less killed, any baby. Maud told me the baby was hers."

Rex started to sing verses from "They All Laughed" again: *"They all laughed at Rockefeller Center, Now they're fighting to get in, They all laughed at Whitney and his cotton gin, They all laughed at Fulton and his steamboat, Hershey and his chocolate bar..."*

"Rex," Marie interrupted, "I want to know your side of things."

"They told Marconi Wireless was phony..."

"Rex," she insisted.

He stopped singing. He said, "She didn't tell you that I was that baby, now did she? She didn't tell you that she, Maud Blake, Nora's sister, is my mother?" He started singing again.

"They all said we never could be happy. They laughed at us and how! But ho, ho, ho! Who's got the last laugh now?"

7

{LOVE}

"My favorite occupation is loving."
—MARCEL PROUST

"Nobody of any stature ever related with whom they slept."
—MARLENE DIETRICH

"Don't eat your heart."
—PYTHAGORAS

Marie's heart was in the middle of performing some sort of arrhythmic jig. She looked at Rex, who was oblivious to her coronary activities. She considered the option of 911, EMS, a DUMBO hospital. She chose instead to ignore it—she wasn't going to let some little heart attack ruin her chance at the biggest story of her career. As the random thudding continued, Marie imagined for herself a substantial raise, name recognition, her own syndicated column. She listened—over the din of her hailstone heart—to a recording of her voice telling New York City cab riders to "buckle up or you'll be a headline in tomorrow's tabloids." She envisioned Miles Brewster winking at her with pride, saying that in his heart of hearts *(thud, thud-thud)* he knew she could deliver the goods and swearing on his mother's grave that he would never ask her to do another rewrite.

Unable to enjoy her imaginary success for very long, Marie began berating herself for not having guessed at the truth earlier. Obviously, only the desire to reveal or suppress a deep dark secret would compel Maud and Rex to keep talking to her. Marie put her hand to her chest. Still, for whatever reason, she was the journalist they were speaking to. At least, she had to give herself some credit for being there, which is not as easy as it would seem. As in any fruitful relationship, hers with Maud and Rex was a case of mutual exploitation. Just how it was working from their end she wasn't sure. Something that was becoming clear, however, was that the deeper she got into this story, the faster her girlhood idol, Nora Mars, became just another human stuck in the dreck of living. *Thud.* Or dying. She felt as if her heart had just jumped off the Empire State Building and landed splat on the sidewalk. As she held her breath and prayed for her heart to get up and walk again, she promised herself that if it did, she would absolutely forsake all lingering fantasies of a tryst with Rex.

Her heart beat, she stood up, walked across the expanse of the loft to the front door, grabbed her knapsack from where she had left it when she came in, and returned to the couch. Rex had made no move to get up, but she had felt his eyes follow-ing her. She took her tape recorder out of her bag, set it on the coffee table in the swank company of the art deco lighter, ash-tray, and cigarette box, and pushed the little red button that said *Record*. She then reached into her bag, found her cell phone, and switched it off as she silently begged Nora to keep her own heart beating at least until the interview with her ex-husband/nephew was over.

"Was the fact that you married your aunt sheer coincidence, or did you know she was your aunt?" Marie bit her lip. It was much too soon to ask that question, but evidently, undermining herself was irresistible. She had tried to keep her voice simply curious, but tiny shards of anger slipped in among her words. She wasn't sure why she was angry or at whom. Rex for de-stroying the myth of Nora. Nora for hurting Rex. Maud for lying to her. Her heart for not beating straight.

Rex didn't respond. He sat with his elbows on his knees and his head in his hands. Marie needed to soften up. She remem-bered one of Nora Mars' notorious quotes pronounced on some talk show not long after she divorced Rex: "Every woman is en-titled to a middle husband she can forget." Marie had always found the line funny but now, sitting face-to-face with that middle husband, the humor was withering. She picked up her glass of water and drained it.

"You wouldn't have anything stronger?" she asked, holding it out toward him. ("When in doubt," Ned Brilliant always said, "drink.")

He got up and walked over to a cabinet against the wall and

brought back a full bottle of Jack Daniel's. "How do you like it?" he asked.

Alcohol never fails with an alcoholic, she thought, then said, "Straight up." Marie took her hand off her heart and ran her palm over the velvet upholstery. She was mildly ashamed of her tactics, but on the other hand she knew that with the help of a little truth serum, from here on in it would be paint-by-number. Nevertheless, she had to be careful. She had to get the story before either of them passed out, or before . . . Marie placed her hand back over her heart and didn't finish the thought.

He filled her glass, then his own, to the rim. Marie took a sip. The whiskey was sweet and sharp. She watched Rex swill his own, dousing that flicker of despair he claimed he lacked the imagination to invent. It came to her that the line Rex had used earlier about unhappiness was said by Charles Boyer in *The Earrings of Madame de . . .,* a wrenching love story made by Max Ophüls in 1953. That movie had always really bothered Marie because the lovers in it—Charles Boyer's wife and another man—are passionately in love, risk everything to be together, end up dying for their love, without ever having had sex. It seemed so unfair. Even Shakespeare allowed Romeo and Juliet to have sex. Or was it Zeffirelli?

Rex sat down in one of the leather armchairs and Marie tried again. "I'm still unclear on how and when you found out you were Maud's son."

"I hired a detective." Rex leaned back and rested the heels of his cowboy boots on the coffee table's glass surface.

"A detective? Why?"

"Have you ever been in love?"

Marie felt herself blush. "You know," she said, looking out the window, "I don't think I ever really have been in love."

Although she had been many times—madly, desperately, wallowing for weeks in Valentine's-Day-candy thoughts like "This is it," "We were made for each other," "It is written in the stars," "I can't live without him," "Two bodies, one soul." There was Mr. Waugh, several movie stars, and her last infatuation fifteen years earlier, Simon Sparks. The problem was he was involved with someone else when she met him and that someone else was her brother, Michael.

("Love is like playing checkers. You have to know which man to move." Nora Mars, *The Labyrinth*, 1973.)

Rex got up and went back to the liquor cabinet, which was part of the curly-maple console, and transformed one end of it into a record player. He placed an LP on the turntable and returned to his chair. Leave it to Rex to be so charmingly retro, Marie thought.

"I was crazy in love. I was obsessed, paranoid, jealous. So I hired a detective—with Nora's money, of course—to tell me her every move."

Marie herself became jealous. And sad. She knew Rex Mars would never feel that crazy about her. She then began calculating: what was the percentage of people who experienced obsessional love in their lives; of that number what was the percentage of people who experienced mutually obsessional love in their lives? She imagined both numbers to be much greater than most people would expect.

Marie settled deeper into the couch and tried to guess what band was playing. Some group from the sixties. She reminded herself to nurse her whiskey, although it was certainly helping to regulate her heart. One might believe, as tall as she was, that she would be able to drink most people under the table, but it wasn't true. "So why did you hire a detective?" she asked.

"As I told you, I was obsessed. I wanted to be with her every second of the day, and, if I couldn't be, I wanted to know where she was at all times." Rex swallowed half his glass of whiskey. "And the more in love I was, the more it seemed Nora lost interest in me, tried to get away from me."

"Funny how that happens," Marie said, distracted by trying to identify the sixties group. "There is probably some law of love equivalent to the principle of conservation of energy: in a system—in this case, two people—the total love is constant. One person will have more, the other less. Two people with infinite love for each other defy the laws of nature and have to cancel each other out, like Romeo and Juliet."

Rex looked confused and Marie couldn't tell if it was because he was high or because she was talking in Marcospeak. In any case, the truth was, when it came to love, Marie was a closet optimist. She believed her one true love was out there somewhere, he would love her as infinitely as she loved him, and they would live happily ever after. When she would meet him was up to fate. In the meantime, just like everyone else, she was drawn toward the Rex Marses of life, the Great Attractors. With a sigh of relief, Marie realized the band they were listening to was the Zombies and that her heart had returned to its usual pace.

She remembered telling Marco, on a foggy Sunday morning at the library, about the Great Attractor. She had been explaining to him that he was wrong about humankind no longer being at the center of things, that, in fact, Einstein proved that we were indeed at the center of the universe—but that so was everything else. According to him, the universe is homogeneous and isotropic, so that no matter where you are in it, it appears as if you are at the center.

"So," said Marco, "it's a democratic universe. We all have equal weight. No need for me to call myself a feminist in the larger scheme of things?"

"Theoretically," she answered, noticing that there was something different about Marco's appearance but she couldn't quite say what it was. "But gravitation—the most mysterious force in the universe—seduces us into believing that there is a hierarchy, a center of things, and the bigger it is, the better it is, as, for example, is the case with the Great Attractor."

"The Great Attractor?" Marco asked rhetorically while fixing her with a bemused stare.

"A supercluster of galaxies that no other galaxy in its vast vicinity can resist. It is 250 million light-years away and contains as many as 500 million galaxies. The Milky Way is headed toward it as we speak and will join the cluster in 50 to 100 billion years. But this is all a matter of perspective. The supercluster appears so huge and massive to us from where we are in the universe. If someone were looking at us from the Great Attractor, who knows what we might look like. Did you see the *Star*'s headline yesterday? HUBBLE SPACECRAFT PHOTO-

GRAPHS HEAVEN PROVING EXISTENCE OF GOD——POPE ASKS NASA FOR COPIES OF THE PICTURES." Marie noticed Marco wasn't reading anything. Maybe that was what was different about him, she thought. "I don't read the *Gotham City Star*," Marco said flatly.

"What do you mean you don't read the *Star*?" Marie was surprised by how hurt she felt. She picked up *Working Mother* and began flipping through its pages. "You read every paper under the sun. Why wouldn't you read the *Star*?" She scrutinized his face again, trying to figure out what had changed.

Marco shrugged his shoulders. "I did read a biography of Chekhov in which the biographer compared Anton's sex life to that of a cheetah."

"A cheetah?" Marie said, wondering what she had triggered now. She tilted her head slightly, the better to hear him.

"Yes. You see, a cheetah can only mate with a stranger. Once intimacy is established, cheetahs cohabit impotently. It seems Chekhov could only have sex with women he didn't particularly know."

"Sounds like a simple case of misogyny to me."

"With cheetahs, both sexes have the same response to intimacy. With humans, evolutionary biologists have led us to believe that women want relationships and not sex, and men want sex and not relationships. The imbalance appears to be not in the sex/intimacy ratio but in the fact that this ratio is unilaterally and inversely assigned to each sex."

Marco began reading *Wound Ballistics Review* while Marie

contemplated Marco's cheetah analogy, which she found rather disturbing. The idea of not having sex with someone she was in love with because they had become too intimate terrified her. She decided then and there that if she ever did get married, she would make a concerted effort not to get to know her husband too well. She put down *Working Mother*.

("Why, when it comes to sexual attraction, is it women who believe that horrible maxim 'mind over matter'? For me it's all matter, matter, matter." Nora Mars, *Lightning*, 1972.)

"But the key to relations between the sexes," Marco said, "is probably not to be found in our ancestral cheetah DNA but in quantum mechanics."

Marie rolled her eyes and smiled indulgently. "Here we go again. You mean the EPR Experiment, Bell's theorem, particles secretly conspiring through some sort of faster-than-light signaling." She looked closely at Marco's blue outfit, which was in fact exquisitely tailored, and debated if it was actually a suit designed by someone like Yohji Yamamoto. She couldn't imagine Marco in a designer suit, but there was a lot that she couldn't imagine about Marco.

"Not exactly," Marco answered, putting down the review. "There's no signaling and there are also no ratios. There is only knowledge and antiknowledge, both maintained simultaneously and accessed at will. I know nothing about you, I know everything about you—both are true."

"And I bet particles have incredible sex lives and the romance never fizzles," Marie said, but wished she hadn't. She wasn't at all sure she wanted to continue having a conversation about sex with Marco. Marie sighed and stood up. "I have no idea why I talk to you instead of working on my paper."

"Because, Marie," Marco said, perusing once again *Wound Ballistics Review,* "you suffer from Bovaryism."

Marie sat back down. "What's that?" She stared at his eyelashes. She never noticed before how long they were.

"The acute belief in the mediocrity of your soul."

"Marco," she said a little too loudly, causing others in the library to look over at them. Marie realized that she almost never said his name out loud. She liked the way it sounded and how it ended in an exclamation. What struck her most was that saying Marco's name made him a little more concrete for her. "That's quite an ailment you've given me."

He leaned toward her, placed his hand on the arm of her chair. "Please, Marie, don't misunderstand me. There is nothing mediocre about you except for your belief that you are mediocre—that's Bovaryism. We all suffer from something or other. I am afflicted with the Emil syndrome."

"The Emil syndrome?"

"Emil from the movie *The Blue Angel,*" Marco explained as Marie picked up and began to read *Euromoney.* "Marlene Dietrich is a nightclub singer named Lola Lola in Berlin," he explained, "and Emil Jannings plays a high school teacher who falls obsessively in love with her. At first she humors him, finds him amusing, is kind to him. She travels around Germany singing with a troupe of musicians and he follows her, does anything to be near her. Marlene begins to be annoyed by him, then disgusted by him. But Emil just becomes more enamored and passionate about her, and at the end of the movie he joins her troupe as a clown so he will never have to leave her."

"How romantic," Marie said, feeling uneasy, as if somehow Marco had guessed about her tendency toward romantic obsession.

"The Emil syndrome," Marco went on, "has little to do with love. As the Irish writer Iris Murdoch once said, 'Love is the extremely difficult realization that something other than oneself is real.' " He then looked at his watch, gathered up his newspapers and magazines, and headed for the elevators. At the time, Marie had been surprised by his abruptness. As he walked away, she had realized what was different about him: his mustache was gone.

Thinking about their conversation now, it was obvious that he had been trying to tell her that it was he who was sick in love with someone. Whoever it was, Marie did not want to know about it. She looked over at Rex, who was gorgeous in the orange light of the setting sun as if he were on a beach in Baja. Although she was loath to admit it, Marco had been right about her Bovaryism. Hadn't Brewster more or less told her the same thing—she didn't want it bad enough? She was content to remain in the realm of the fearful. And here she was, probably blowing the biggest story she'd ever get lucky enough to stumble upon because she suffered not only from Bovaryism but even worse from the Emil syndrome. She got up and went over to Rex. His empty glass was clutched in his hands and resting on his chest. His eyes were closed and the Zombies were singing, "The only cure for loving is loving even more."

She leaned over him and was about to press her lips to his ear when she suddenly realized that Rex had quite possibly passed out. She glanced around the room to make sure no one had witnessed her near lapse in judgment. Hadn't years of movie watching taught her that only a true heel would make love to someone under the influence of alcohol? If she and Rex were ever to embark on a romance, would she really want it all to begin under these circumstances? In any case, she had to get the story out of him before he sank any deeper into his stupor. She walked over to the wall of windows and opened all of them as wide as they would go. She could just imagine herself explaining to Brewster how she got Rex Mars drunk so that he would talk, but, because she was so preoccupied with lusting after the middle-aged ballad singer with bulging biceps, she had allowed him to lose consciousness before she got the story. She'd never live it down.

"So, Rex," Marie said loudly, sitting down in the chair next to his, "back to the detective. How did he find out that Maud Blake was your mother?"

Rex sat up, the glass fell to the floor. He picked it up, rubbed his eyes, filled the glass with whiskey. "It was Melanie's idea," he said. "Melanie Diaz. The detective was a woman." He drank long. "The agency recommended I use a female operative to follow my wife. They said it was more efficient, less surreptitious."

By the way he said Melanie's name, Marie was sure they

had slept together. She could imagine the entire scenario: They talk daily on the telephone, meet for lunch. After reporting on Nora's activities she asks for his life story. She feels sorry for him, wants to help him, and he's good-looking. She then finds out the awful truth, comforts him, and one thing leads to another. So reductive, Marie thought, so true.

"We got to talking," Rex said. "I told her that my whole life I had always felt as if I didn't fit in, didn't belong anywhere, until I met Nora. I mentioned that maybe it was because I had been adopted as an infant. She asked me if I had ever found out who my parents were. I told her I never thought it was an option."

Rex's words were beginning to slur slightly, as they had at the Ear Inn. He sounded tired or sad, but not drunk, which he was.

"It turns out that Melanie's true specialty as a detective was investigating the birth parents of adoptees. It took her a week to find out who my mother was and another week to decide how to tell me about it. I was shocked—and disgusted."

"Well," said Marie, her own shock plus alcohol and dope making her flippant. "It's not as if Nora were your mother. Besides, even Jocasta and Oedipus were married for years, had a swell time together, even had four healthy kids before finding out the ugly truth. You really shouldn't feel so bad."

"It's still incest, Marie," Rex said, looking at Marie as if she had come from outer space. He then added with more conviction, "Don't pretend that tabloid blood of yours isn't screaming with delighted horror and shame."

Rex's telephone rang somewhere at the other end of the loft. Marie jolted up. Her knees hit the coffee table. The whiskey bottle, nearly empty, toppled over but didn't spill. Her first thought was that Nora was dead. As Rex sauntered off to find the phone, she prayed feverishly for Nora's life.

("I don't pray—it's bad for the knees." Nora Mars, *Evil Love*, 1962.)

It occurred to her, however, that the probability was high that the person on the other end of the line was another journalist. Rex was too far away for her to hear the conversation, but she realized that no matter whom he was talking to, she wouldn't have him to herself for much longer. When he got off the phone, he went to the windows and began closing them. Outside, it was near dark, the air was cooler, and the city was just starting to flick on its lights.

"Rex," Marie said, joining him at the windows, "maybe we should clarify some things. Why exactly are you telling me all this? I mean, aren't you supposed to be writing a memoir? Why are you letting me scoop you? And why now?" she asked. "Why are you talking about all this now?"

"I didn't bring it up." Rex stared at Marie, his green eyes vague and glistening. "You did." He put a finger under her chin and tilted her head slightly back. She saw herself fainting from his touch, toppling over backward. He leaned very near to her face so that she could feel the heat of his breath, smelling of whiskey and dope. "If all this is going to be common knowledge, I just want to have my say." He turned away from her. "I'll never write any memoir," he said, picking up the whiskey bottle and draining it. "Can't you tell just by looking at me that I'll never finish it? I am the ex-husband of a movie star that I never even fucked." He sat back down on the armchair and lit another joint.

Stunned, Marie said nothing. Nora and Rex hadn't even had sex? Was that better or worse? Was the tragedy greater having had sex or not having had it? Or was it really only a matter of how we looked at it? Zeffirelli vs. Ophüls; cheetahs vs. humans; Nora vs. Rex. In her own case, she'd only had sex with Simon once, yet the one drunken transgression had caused her brother not to speak to her for fifteen years. On the other hand, she'd had years of illicit sex with Ned and it didn't seem to change a thing for anyone, his wife included. From what Marie understood, his wife was having her own affair, she and Ned loved each other, and they wanted to have a family together. She had always found the rules governing sex and love extraordinarily strange, their implications profoundly puzzling. She sat on the couch and took the joint Rex was holding out to her. She inhaled, hoping the marijuana would take effect quickly and give her brain a short vacation.

"You can write whatever you like, Marie, but if you print that little fact, I'll kill you. It was so completely humiliating for me." He lay back in the chair. "Here was this woman I adored and she tortured me by never letting me touch her."

"She must have known she was your aunt," Marie said, handing him back the joint, still not sure why exactly that would have made a difference. She was not advocating incest— but wasn't the real damage done when Nora *married* Rex?

"Yeah, it's likely. Melanie was convinced of it. But I had no idea. I just thought I was the luckiest guy in the world and then felt like the most rejected guy in the world." After taking another couple of hits he tossed the joint into the ashtray. "What a weird, fucked-up thing for her to do. But you want to know the really sick thing? After I found out she was my aunt, I only wanted her more." Marie understood what he meant—although it was hard for her to think about, she knew that her fierce attraction to Simon had been fueled by the fact that he was involved with her brother.

("To be is to be related." Nora Mars, *No Ordinary Matter*, 1958.)

"But she wanted nothing to do with me," Rex continued. "I was so angry I almost went public and revealed the whole thing. But I didn't because I had the creepy feeling that she would have reveled in it somehow. I guess finally it was Melanie who convinced me that I should just move on, that talking to the press might let me enjoy a few hours of revenge but that I would end up getting far more hurt than I had been already."

Marie laid her head back on the armrest, her left ear toward Rex. She could no longer see his mouth, but if she missed anything, she could rely on the tape recorder. She wondered, briefly, what had happened to Melanie.

"I always had the feeling," Rex went on, his voice even and slow, "that I was being used, that I was a minor player in a real life psychodrama starring Nora and Maud. Finally, the last act has begun and it appears you, Marie, have walked onstage."

"A post-Freudian Hollywood version of The Weird Sisters," Marie said to the ceiling. She saw an image of Nora and Maud, tall and drop-dead beautiful, wearing black silk strapless evening gowns and tall cone-shaped black hats. Between them, a huge black cauldron billowed green smoke as they used their ivory and onyx inlaid broomsticks to stir the brew. In the smoke rising from the large pot, Marie just barely made out the image of Rex's face, but it was distorted and ghostly and had nothing of his rugged good looks. She closed her eyes. "Rex," she said, unsure how she was going to drag herself out of his loft, much less drive home, "I want you to know that I am deeply sorry for any pain I've caused you by dredging up all this stuff."

He didn't respond or at least Marie hadn't heard him if he did. When she next opened her eyes, he was gone from the chair. A light was on at the far end of the loft. The curtain around the bed was open and Rex was lying facedown on it, still wearing his cowboy boots. The next move was hers.

8

{ R E A L I T Y }

"Nothing is real."
—JOHN LENNON

"I'm so sick of Nancy Drew, I could vomit."
—MILDRED BENSON

"The only existing things are atoms and empty space;
all else is mere opinion."
—DEMOCRITUS OF ABDERA

As Marie approached the cream-colored 1959 Chevy Impala convertible early the following morning, a flash of bright orange caught her eye. A parking ticket had been neatly folded and stuffed into the crack between the hood and the frame of the car. A young man in a suit and tie carrying a portfolio hurried past her and an older couple snapped photographs of each other standing in front of a warehouse; otherwise the street was empty of people—as if she had been transported to the downtown of some industrial midwestern city on a Sunday. It was, in fact, a Sunday, she thought, and whoever heard of getting a ticket on a Sunday? Only in New York City. She extracted the ticket, leaned against a bat wing fender, and carefully unfolded it.

Marie saw three ways to interpret this message. The first and most appealing was to see the ticket as a kind of love letter, an affirmation of her willingness to follow her desire and to take risks. How would she ever find true love if she didn't take risks? The second and the more predictable reading was to see the ticket as an omen. She had made a mistake by being so unprofessional as to get stoned and drunk with Rex Mars that she passed out in his apartment and stayed the night. One way or another she was going to pay for the transgression, although, in all fairness, it could have been a whole lot worse. The third, and hardest, interpretation to bear, due to its utter lack of meaning, was that she had parked illegally and received notification of the fine corresponding to the infraction. Whichever of the three she chose, it was going to cost her fifty-five dollars. She decided it was time to return the car.

When she opened the car door, she saw a package neatly wrapped in newspaper lying on the passenger seat. She had the fleeting notion that it was a present from Rex; that he had woken up at the crack of dawn, found her keys, snuck out to her car, and left her a small remembrance of their emotional evening together. She quickly realized, however, that the package contained the three hexagonal blue bottles Marie had bought from the Russian woman the day before—an event that by now seemed so long ago as to be part of another lifetime. Sometimes, Marie thought, her imagination was just plain ridiculous.

The day was already warm, so Marie took the roof down in order to enjoy to their fullest her last moments with the Impala. She had difficulty finding her way out of DUMBO and onto the Manhattan Bridge. She could see precisely where she needed to go—the bridge loomed overhead—but could determine no way to get there. Twice she wound up at a dead end. The second time she realized in a moment of terror that her cell phone was off. She grabbed it out of the side pocket of her backpack, sure she would find a message from Brewster telling her Nora Mars had died in the middle of the night. Her voice mail was empty. A little too empty. She put in a call to St. Vincent's for an update on Nora's condition and was told by a volunteer making yawning sounds that the actress was still in intensive care.

Only when Marie finally made it onto the bridge, Manhattan running toward her with outstretched arms, did she let herself imagine the look on Brewster's face when she gave him the lowdown on Rex and Nora Mars. She mulled over Rex's request that she omit the fact that the marriage was never consummated. Of course, it was in her interest to do so, since, as Rex rightly pointed out, incest made for greater scandal. She decided to respect Rex's wishes, for the moment anyway. When she left the loft, he was still lying facedown on his bed with his boots on. She debated if he would be relieved or disappointed when he woke up and found her gone. Or worse, if he would even remember that she had been there. She wondered what forces had aligned to prevent her from slipping between Rex's sheets last night.

Coming off the bridge, she made a wrong turn and was forced onto Canal Street. The sidewalks were thick with vendors of everything from vegetables and fish to clothing and electronics. And because it was Sunday, this huge and teeming outdoor market was crawling with tourists. Marie sat in front of Henry DuLee's House of Diamonds crunched between delivery trucks and breathing exhaust fumes for nearly fifteen minutes. Above the jewelry store was a wedding-gown showroom. One-stop shopping. Of all the made-to-order fantasies life had to offer, Marie marveled at the persistence of the bride fantasy in the psyches of all women, rich or poor, tall or short, fat or thin, smart or dumb. Was it chromosomal or just good marketing?

("If you're thinking about getting me a diamond, make sure it looks like it belongs in a highball." Nora Mars, *Dark Blue*, 1965.)

The overwhelming probability for Marie, however, given her age and temperament, was that she would never swirl through a day in a white dress, flash her chunk of ice at the appreciative, bask in the envy of the unmarried, but she held on to the possibility, and thanks to the new field of quantum cosmology and the multiverse theory—which says that everything that can happen really does happen, but often in other universes—in a parallel universe she'd done it, lived the whole thing. She was married now with three kids, a loving (rich) husband, a beautiful house in a town with excellent schools, two Volvos, a dog, a complete wardrobe mail-ordered from Neiman-Marcus, family vacations in Sweden and Sicily, no fewer than sixty pairs of shoes. In some other spacetime she was living this and loving every second of it.

A truck honked and through the din she heard a man's voice yell, "Put the pedal to the metal, princess."

Marie turned up Mulberry Street and envisioned her well-shod suburban self popping Xanax in between hourly wine-tasting sessions. As she headed toward the East Village to return the car, she ruminated about herself and Rex and why she felt the need to project their entire future together. Would Rex ever even think of doing such a thing? But even more to the point, Rex was hardly the man of her Volvo-driven dreams. The reality was that if they ever did get together, she'd move to DUMBO (the bigger apartment), spend a few years unpacking Rex's emotional baggage, at which point he would be diagnosed with prostate cancer and lose his already waning virility. They would never own a car. She wondered why reality always had to be so harsh, causing humans to waste so much time and effort trying to escape it.

("Reality is something you rise above." Nora Mars, *The Labyrinth*, 1973.)

Not long ago, on a Monday morning, Brewster, wearing a bow tie sporting little pink pigs with wings flying across a royal-blue background, dumped four rewrites on her minutes after announcing the promotion of a junior reporter—male and short and hired two years after she was—to a senior editorial position. As Brewster bestowed upon her the offending articles, she experienced what could be described as an overdose of reality. In response, she left the *Star* offices then and there and headed for the Science, Industry and Business Library in search of Marco Trentadue, freelance intellectual.

Marie had always prided herself on her *Emperor's New Clothes* realism. She believed, no matter how painful it might be, in calling a spade a spade. She saw Marco, on the other hand, as one of the weavers—a knave, a rogue, spinning his own reality, seeing what he wanted to see, with no regard whatsoever for the concept of truth. But there was something oddly reassuring about him. His total lack of interest in reality made her feel more sure about her own firm handle on it. Being with Marco, as frustrating and annoying as he could be, she often felt herself undergo a kind of renormalization process. It was as if he were some sort of virtual photon with an infinite number of contributions. By adjusting herself ever so slightly to one of his contributions, she could cancel out all the other realities that were invading her own and making her feel out of control. "Marcospeak," she said to herself, shaking her head, as she hurried through the front entrance of the library. To put it much more simply, she thought, Marco was so nuts that, by contrast, he made her feel less nuts.

As she passed through the lobby on her way downstairs to the reading room, she imagined she was strolling through B. Altman's ground floor, admiring counters cluttered with lipsticks, liners, and creams, ogling display cases overflowing with jewels and silks. Saleswomen offered to make her over and spray her with perfume that would allegedly cause any man to fall before her and beg to be stepped on. In reality, the library lobby was soaring and spare and she was alone in it apart from the man behind the information desk.

Downstairs, the reading room was nearly empty. A woman in a business suit sat in front of a stack of annual reports at one of the cubicles. Two androgynous teenagers with blond shoulder-length hair whispered to each other over by the reference stacks. A handsome young Asian man in the front lounge area drew in a sketchbook. Marie circled the floor but Marco was nowhere to be found. She looked in the computer room, the microform center, the cubicles behind the chemical-abstract shelves. She wasn't sure what she would say to him if she did find him: "I'm in need of a relative reality cure. My reality sucks but compared to yours it's nirvana."

She walked over to the large glass elevator that would take her back up to the lobby and end this sick mission. She pressed the button and the doors opened immediately. She stared into the empty square but didn't step inside. The doors closed. She pushed the button again, the elevator doors opened, she waited until the doors closed without stepping inside.

She decided to take one last spin around the floor. She walked behind the artist and looked over his shoulder. He was drawing a comic strip featuring spaceships and aliens. She moved on through the chemical abstracts and came upon the teenagers she had seen whispering earlier, now seated on the floor making out. In the computer room a towheaded girl no older than ten was moving chess pieces across a computer screen. Marie crossed the reading room and went into the microform center. Marco was lying on his side on the floor beneath a microfilm machine in his navy-blue pajama suit, his head perched on a hand, reading. He looked so comfortable, so at home, that it recrossed her mind that Marco might live in the library. Several newspapers and magazines were spread out on the floor in front of him. The machine he lay under was on and the blank screen projected a luminous square above his head.

"I was just thinking about you," Marco said, looking up, a pleasantly surprised grin spread across his wide mouth.

"You were?" Marie asked. She suddenly felt a little paranoid and a little guilty that Marco knew her purpose in finding him. "What about?"

"I wanted to get your opinion on the Copenhagen interpretation," he explained, and Marie relaxed, a slight smile of relief coming to her lips.

Ostensibly, Marie's quantum paper was centered on Niels Bohr's 1927 Copenhagen interpretation of the quantum world that said, basically, that fundamental particles exist as ghostly superpositions where they can be, say, in a billion different places at once or in a billion different states. Only when observed by a conscious being do they choose one of these places or states in which to become "real." The question Marie was having so much trouble with in her paper was: what does this mean for our view of reality—if anything? Physicists, philosophers, literary theorists, had all grappled with the question and no one could agree, so it was the perfect mind-blowing first-year-graduate-school term-paper assignment. Marie was beginning to realize that for her it had triggered a fifteen-year paralysis of sorts.

"I was reading an article yesterday about the recent discovery of these huge bursts of gamma radiation coming from the edge of the universe," Marco said. He stood up and brushed himself off and they headed for their usual chairs in the reading room. "It seems these bursts are more proof that ours may not be the only universe but one of perhaps an infinite number of universes." His excitement was palpable and Marie was enjoying listening to him explore this new territory. But she was afraid of making him self-conscious by appearing to listen too closely to what he was saying, so she picked up a movie magazine called *Real to Reel* and pretended to read it as he continued talking. "The article said that this was all predicted, based on discoveries in particle physics, in 1927 by Niels Bohr in the Copenhagen interpretation."

Marie was eager to hear where Marco was going to wind up with this one.

"So correct me here if I'm wrong. A particle keeps all its options, all its probabilities, open for as long as possible. It is our observation of the particle that forces it to select one of its options, which then becomes real. As soon as we stop looking at the particle, it immediately splits up into a new array of ghost particles, each pursuing its own path."

Marie looked up from her magazine and added with feigned indifference, "And for Bohr it wasn't just ghost particles that were conjured out of the quantum equations, but ghost realities, ghost worlds, ghost universes, that existed when we weren't looking at them."

"Well, then," he went on, obviously pleased with himself for what he was about to tell her, "doesn't the Copenhagen interpretation place us more at the center of things than ever before? Doesn't it mean that with each scientific revolution—Copernicus, Galileo, Newton, Darwin, Einstein, Hubble—it was actually an illusion that humankind was moving away from the center of things and toward some sort of objective reality where we were just a tiny speck in the grand plan? It appears that the more we discover about the physical world, the more it becomes clear that we are actually moving more absolutely toward the center of things in an observer-dependent universe where our observations make the world real."

Marie said nothing. Hadn't she come to the library for this? She had fled Brewster and her stalled career at the *Star* in order to seek out Marco and his special brand of escapism, which he was now offering her. Why, when she got what she wanted, did she not want it anymore?

("It is the nature of desire not to be satisfied." Nora Mars, *Checkmate*, 1971.)

"So is it fair to say," Marco asked, "that our present theory of nature—quantum mechanics—infers that it's all in the mind, that our reality is what we choose to perceive? Our separate realities may mesh or clash, but fundamentally reality is a consensual agreement among the lot of us."

Marie sighed. Marco was determined to come up with some grassroots version of Max Born's quantum theory of human affairs. Marco had been enthralled by the Sokal hoax. He still believed that Alan Sokal's paper on the postmodern cross-pollination of cultural studies and science, especially the inference from quantum physics to Jacques Lacan's psychoanalytic ideas, was quite simply brilliant. He refused to accept that the paper was a parody. His reaction was akin to someone reading Jonathan Swift's *A Modest Proposal* and then declaring that we should all start eating babies. He missed the point entirely.

"That is just one interpretation," Marie finally answered. "In fact, this observer question is what led to the notorious spat between Einstein and Bohr. Einstein insisted that our observations merely uncover the reality that already exists, whereas Bohr says that our observations actually create that reality. In 1964, Bell's theorem mathematically demonstrated that no local explanation can account for the known facts of quantum mechanics."

Marco looked at her blankly. "What's a local explanation?"

"A local explanation is one that assumes that things seemingly separate in space and time are really separate," Marie explained, finding herself yet again pronouncing on things that were entirely mysterious to her. But she couldn't help herself from becoming excited by the material—by, as Michael had once upon a time pointed out, its metaphor. She was, however, very glad that only Marco was listening to her. "It assumes, for example, that time and space are independent of our nervous systems, our consciousness. According to Bell's theorem, in quantum mechanics that assumption is simply not valid. The whole idea of separation is questionable."

"I see," said Marco. He raised his hand toward his goatee in order to pull on it, but then didn't. "The emotional component of this quantum mechanics is entirely compelling."

Marie rolled her eyes. "Bell's theorem was later upheld by the Aspect Experiment, carried out in 1982, which involved a pair of photons and their polarization—remember your entangled particles?"

Marco nodded. "How could I forget?"

She ignored him and went on. "Einstein said that polarization is a property independent of observation. The experiment proved that photons do not determine their polarization until detected. And, even more amazing, the observation of one photon will determine the polarization of the other instantaneously and no matter how far apart they are—it's known as quantum teleportation. And some interpretations of quantum mechanics insist that all particles in the universe are somehow connected."

"Oh, my," Marco said quietly.

"For me the experience of thinking about this stuff is like looking at an Escher print or a Magritte painting—at first I find it disturbing, unfathomable, suffocating, but, as I keep staring, I move from seeing the painting from the outside to being inside the painting, and from within it is endlessly fascinating, a world that is at once sealed off and infinite." The library, and Marco himself, she thought, had a similar effect on her, but she wouldn't have dreamed of saying that aloud in a billion years.

"But the bottom line is this," she added quickly, coming back to the real world. "Even though for practical purposes physics now relies heavily on quantum mechanics, most physicists simply ignore its theoretical implications, considering them too murky or as Einstein said too 'spooky' to be acceptable as the final description of our reality. And a majority of the physicists who don't ignore the paradoxes of quantum mechanics are avidly trying to replace quantum mechanics with observer-*independent* theories."

She looked at her watch, knowing she should get back to the office.

"Do you suppose," Marco asked, "our minds can't quite grasp the excitement of it?"

Marie coughed. "The excitement of what?"

"A reality in which we have collectively created the entire universe."

"Okay, that's it," Marie said, standing up. "My reality is this: I've got four articles to write for which I'll get no credit. I've been yet again passed over for a promotion. I spend hours in this library talking gibberish to you and writing a paper I will never finish. In this universe my life has been one long series of mistakes."

While she was talking Marco had picked up *Cigar Aficionado*. She had left the library and gone back to the *Star* without bothering to say good-bye to him.

But mistakes could actually be wonderful things, Marie was thinking as she pulled the Impala into the High-Low Cars garage. Because she had been given the wrong car, she'd gotten to spend a whole weekend whizzing around in the driver's seat of a swank convertible, living out one of her myriad movie-star fantasies, all the while pursuing a story that could make tabloid history. On the other hand, she was also a little glad to be giving up the car. It wasn't exactly her. She was beginning to feel as if she didn't know anymore—or perhaps never had known—what was exactly her.

("Among all your possible lives, you have to anchor yourself to one to be able to have the most fun in all the others." Nora Mars, *The Labyrinth*, 1973.)

When she walked into the High-Low Cars office, a tall man who looked alarmingly like her brother, Michael, but with less hair was talking to the same gum-chewing receptionist. She was blowing the most amazing double, triple, quadruple bubbles. *Pop pop. Pop pop pop. Pop pop pop pop.*

"Michael?" Marie asked, hoping to God it wasn't he. This was not the time or the place for their first encounter after fifteen years.

He turned toward her and blushed a deep velvety red. It happened whenever Michael was surprised. Marie decided that "fate" was no longer the sexiest word in the English language, but the cruelest. She heard a loud multiple *pop. Pop pop pop.* "She's the one," the woman said, pointing a finger at Marie. "She took your car."

"Marie," he said flatly, "what a coincidence."

Marie remembered that when Michael was a senior in high school, he read Arthur Koestler's book on parapsychology, and came up with a theory that coincidence was an archaic remnant from a time when humans communicated telepathically. Such intimate knowledge of others' psyches had proved dangerous to the survival of the species—people became so involved and excited exploring each other's brains that they stopped eating, sleeping, having children. Evolution had responded by getting rid of telepathy. Traces of its former existence, Michael claimed, could still be found in phenomena such as coincidences. He believed that attempts to re-create the primal neurocommunal state produced theater, then books, movies, and television. A tragic and as-yet-unresolved outcome of this evolutionary step, Michael concluded, was that humans were forced to rely on the entirely inadequate tool of language to communicate and have therefore remained a profoundly lonely species.

("Coincidence is an extraordinary thing because it is so natural." Nora Mars, *The Affair*, 1963.)

During high school and then throughout college, probably in an effort to fight loneliness, she and Michael would spend hours discussing the Big Questions. And from those interminable talks emerged the Four Grand (insoluble) Enigmas:

1. *Is death the end of being or only an unknown transformation?*
2. *Does mind depend on matter or matter on mind?*
3. *Does the world obey a law, or is it only a chaos in which forces clash at random?*
4. *Is there a purpose to life or is it merely an accident?*

Pop pop.

"I didn't know you were in New York," Marie said, as if he had simply forgotten to tell her. "What brings you East?"

"I came for a wedding. I was supposed to drive the bride and groom from the church to the reception in the Impala."

"Are you still peddling your stories to the movies?" she asked, feeling guilty, of all things, for having hijacked the Impala and Michael's friend's wedding.

"Yup," he said, signing the credit-card slip.

Pop.

"Do you want to go get some coffee or something?" Marie asked, wondering when they were going to quit the small talk and say something real to each other. They were, after all, coauthors of the Four Grand (insoluble) Enigmas. That had to count for something.

"Can't," he said, folding the credit-card receipt into his wallet. "I gotta go. I'm late."

"You're never late," she said. "I miss you, Michael."

"Yeah, well," he said, shrugging his shoulders, heading for the door. He stopped just before it, turned to face Marie, and said with no sound, only his lips, "I have cut you out of my life like a bruise from an apple." He then walked out the door for, she thought, another fifteen years, twenty, forever?

She considered running after him, begging him to forgive her, to help her figure out some way they could know each other again. But she couldn't bear another rejection, or to see in every faint line on his face all the pain she had caused him.

Marie walked up to the counter and handed the woman the keys to the Impala.

"The guy who just left," the woman asked, "the guy who was supposed to get the Impala, you know him?" *Pop, pop pop.*

"Yes."

"Just sign here," she said, pointing at a dotted line at the bottom of a form. "Ex-husband?" she asked.

"No, no," Marie said, signing. "Brother."

Pop, pop.

She heard the opening chords of Cole Porter's "I've Got You Under My Skin" emanating from the side pocket of her backpack.

"Yes?" she said, answering her cell phone.

"She's dead." It was Brewster.

"When?"

"A few minutes ago."

Marie fought the overwhelming urge to divulge everything to Brewster. She wanted to tell him that her brother, whom she hadn't seen in fifteen years, had just walked in and out of her life in a two-minute span while she stood in the tropically scented office of High-Low Cars being observed by a woman blowing Olympic-class bubbles. She wanted to confess to him that she had driven an expensive car all weekend, that she'd come very close to having sex with Rex Mars, that she'd passed out while on the job. She wanted to tell Brewster that she shouldn't have asked to do this story in the first place, that he was right she didn't want it bad enough, that she didn't deserve ever to fall in love.

"I'm on my way," she said.

Pop.

9

{ DEATH }

*"This I know, that no one has ever died who was
not destined to die sometime."*
—ST. AUGUSTINE

"Excuse my dust."
—DOROTHY PARKER

*"The neutrino is at the very edge between
existence and nonexistence."*
—LEON M. LEDERMAN

Hideous traffic caused Marie's cab ride from the High-Low
Cars office to the *Star* to take nearly half an hour when it
should have taken less than ten minutes. The anxiety involved
in being late, Marie decided, was far more stressful than the by-
comparison-almost-enjoyable litany of self-deprecation that
came with being early. When she was early, at least she knew

what she was up against. When she was late, the possible consequences were incalculable. So far she had imagined Brewster murdering her with the pistol he kept in his desk, firing her, giving the obituary to someone else to write. She realized that this incalculability, this state of not having an inkling of the outcome, made her feel both excited and crazy. She looked to the Empire State Building for courage as she rushed into the *Star* offices. Brewster was sitting at her desk with all her file drawers open and her computer on.

"I gave you a break on this one, Brown," he said, nervously fingering his pink-and-purple-paisley bow tie. "I could have given the story to Sonny or Trudy but, I thought, since she asked, let's give Marie a chance to show her stuff." Marie knew Brewster was upset because his usually well-coiffed snow-white hair was looking Einsteinian. "But what do I get? Not the right stuff, not the wrong stuff, no fucking stuff at all. I can't find the Mars obituary anywhere." He waved his hands dismissively around her cubicle.

From her backpack, Marie pulled out a fuchsia-colored floppy. "It's right here," she said, waving it at him. "I keep it close to my heart because I am afraid of snoops and moles. Remember, you can never be too rich, too thin, or too paranoid."

Brewster scowled. "You have until two o'clock to put the deep dark truth about Nora Mars on my desk. And if it isn't stellar stuff, you're out."

Brewster had never spoken to her like that before. He'd always been falsely obsequious with her, as if he thought she didn't deserve the energy of demand or anger. She couldn't believe he had just threatened to fire her—that was something he did only to the senior staff he most prized. She glanced out the window at the 102-floor art-deco eighth wonder of the world and silently thanked her for being there.

"I need the late-edition deadline," Marie said, spinning her Rolodex for the number of the Excelsior Hotel. Her cab anxiety had left her and suddenly she felt like Clark Kent. The late-edition deadline was reserved for breaking stories about presidents' assassinations, wars involving at least one Western country, and—above all, sex scandals. Her story qualified in the latter category even if it was a bit cobweb-covered.

"You need what?" Brewster said, standing.

"You give me the seven-P.M. deadline and I'll not only give you the stars, I'll give you a front-page supernova." Marie's hubris was impressing—and terrifying—even herself.

Out of his breast pocket, Brewster took a little red notebook he called his pacemaker. It was where, throughout the day, he jotted and jostled the next day's possible cover stories.

"Are you telling me"—Brewster was winking at her so furiously she thought he must be seeing her in strobe—"that you think what you've got merits more than a front-page leader? You actually want space?"

Marie nodded, and stared right into his eyes until much to her surprise he stopped winking.

"You've got it."

If Marie hadn't been standing, she would have fallen out of her proverbial chair. Brewster was giving her a front page and she hadn't even fed him the meat of the story yet. It was too good to be true. Had her time simply come? Is this how it happens? You just get a break one day and your life changes forever? She decided tomorrow's lineup must be really bad. Probably all Brewster had was another cheesy profile of one of the city's homeless. He had learned that 90 percent of the population with an income higher than $100,000 a year feared homelessness as much as Cancer and Alzheimer's, so he started a series of articles called "There Go I," describing the life paths of random street people. The series began as back-of-the-book human-interest filler but became so successful that it was now regular front-page fare. But there had been a few too many of those recently and readers were weary. The time was ripe for the death of a movie star and the glamorous scandals that had riddled her life, and Marie would give it to the *Star*'s readers on the front page. She suddenly became deeply concerned for the president's safety. It would be just her luck for him to go and get himself assassinated.

Brewster peered at Marie. "You better not be bluffing, Brown. Let me just remind you that you are a hack and no matter how good you might get you will never be Walter Winchell. You've got until six to get me the story and it better not be a white dwarf."

Left alone, Marie called the Excelsior Hotel. Before she started writing up the final version of the Nora Mars story, she wanted to talk to Maud Blake one more time—if at all possible—and get a confirmation or a denial of Rex's story. The chances were slim that Maud would be in her hotel room at noon on the day her sister died. On the other hand . . .

("The dead look so terribly dead when they're dead." Nora Mars, *The End of Sarah*, 1973.)

She asked to be connected to Maud's room. While the phone rang and rang she tried again to conceive of Nora Mars as actually being dead, but she was having a hard time. Nora Mars just did not feel dead to Marie in the same sense that she had never really felt alive to her either. And even though the people in the diva's life were becoming very real to Marie, Nora herself still belonged in some other category encompassing neither the living nor the dead.

Someone picked up on the other end. "No comment." It was Maud's voice. She hung up.

Marie pressed *Redial*. She prayed that for whatever reason Maud, who must have been receiving calls from the press all morning, hadn't talked. Her "no comment" was a good indication that she hadn't. The phone rang for an eternity. Finally, Maud picked up. "No—"

"Maud, it's Marie Brown. Rex told me that you are his mother and I want to hear about it from you."

There was a silence, then a sigh. "I've been fighting off hordes of rabid tabloiders for hours. I don't know why I should talk to you over any of them. Besides," she said mockingly, "I can't imagine how they found out where I was staying."

Marie glanced around the room. Who is the mole? she wondered. Dick Penrose, Raquelle Goode, Abraham Singh? Her eyes landed on Edith Quick's chignon. Marie remembered hearing there was something brewing between Edith and Ned Brilliant. And Edith *had* seemed rather over eager to help her on Nora Mars' obituary. "Do you think I'd hand you over to the competition? You must know by now that I see you and your sister as my ticket to the big time," Marie said.

Maud chuckled. "So how did you get it out of him? The whole thing is such a devastating embarrassment to him. Did you get him drunk? Sleep with him? No, let me guess—both."

Marie let the air out of her lungs. "Anything to get the story," she said, waited a few beats, then added, "The paper goes to bed in a few hours. Will you talk to me?"

"I'm on my way to the American Museum of Natural History across the street here. I wanted to see some dead things in their natural habitats. Meet me in front of the yaks in fifteen minutes."

Marie grabbed her backpack and her fuchsia floppy and ran for the elevator. Yaks—Maud was making fun of her but what did Marie care as long as she talked? In the best of all possible worlds, Marie estimated, it would take her fifteen minutes in a cab to get from the *Star* to the museum. Perhaps her days of being early were over.

"Where the fuck do you think you're going?" Brewster asked as she sped past. Probably looking for the daily odds at Aqueduct, he was hunched over the desk of Dick Penrose, the sports editor.

"To Mars via wormhole," she yelled.

Once out on the street, she saw the traffic was still bumper-to-bumper—she'd have to take the B train from Herald Square. A policewoman rode by on a chestnut mare and Marie imagined herself as ace reporter Nellie Bly, hijacking the horse and galloping away up Fifth Avenue and across Central Park in pursuit of the story. Walter Winchell, Marie scoffed as she dashed to the subway entrance under Macy's: who wanted to be that old cigar-smoking cynic? She'd rather be Nellie Bly any day.

The subway came immediately, and it was a straight shot, which meant she'd probably get there on time after all. During her ride, she tried to formulate what exactly to say to Maud. Was there a delicate way to convince a woman whose famous sister had just died that their well-kept family secrets would be best served as tabloid fodder? Marie was hanging onto a pole, towering over the man standing next to her, who was chattering away to a woman who was sitting reading a *New Yorker*. The man was wearing a T-shirt that said "Life is short, make fun of it." A homeless woman walked down the aisle holding out a McDonald's coffee cup asking for change. Marie remembered the guy in the pizza place in DUMBO and gave the woman a dollar. The woman said nothing to Marie but thanked an old man profusely when he gave her his half-eaten ice cream. The guy in the T-shirt said to the seated woman still reading her magazine, "Anyway, I was innocent." When the car cleared out at Fifty-ninth Street, Marie found herself staring at a photograph of five giraffes. Large red print running across the bottom of the advertisement read GET A NEW PERSPECTIVE AT THE BRONX ZOO.

When Marie emerged from the subway, the overcast sky had darkened considerably and the air appeared to be some sort of gray and glowing ether. She took the steps two at a time up to the front door of the Natural History Museum. By the time she'd paid her entrance fee and found the yak exhibit in the Asian mammals section, her entire trip had miraculously taken only fourteen minutes. The stars were aligning for her, she thought.

Marie waited for twenty minutes while two large, hairy, horned, and stuffed yaks stared out at her from behind glass. A group of children, paired off and holding hands, walked by. One small boy asked his partner, "How does the yak go?" The girl, who had bright orange hair, began snorting loudly. The children erupted into laughter, which made the snorter intensify her performance.

Maud, it appeared, had pulled a fast one. Her hotel was across the street—she should have long since been there to meet Marie. Maud probably never had any intention of talking to Marie in the first place and made the appointment at the museum just to get rid of her. Maybe she had even decided to betray Marie and talk to other reporters. So much for star alignment. She thought of the harsh tone Brewster had taken with her earlier. Perhaps she had misinterpreted him and he really didn't have any confidence in her as a journalist—he'd simply been setting her up so that he could fire her. And he would be right, she thought. She'd been conned by Maud, sent on a wild-yak chase. She then started up her old familiar litany—she was still tall, still deaf, still unmarried, still a graduate school dropout, still writing for a tabloid—but somehow the list just wasn't compelling enough to continue.

At first Marie thought she was seeing a ghost. The striking similarity between sisters was already unnerving, but today it was as if Maud, in some macabre homage to her sister, had chosen to dress up as Nora. She was wearing gray silk slacks and a short light gray cashmere jacket with large buttons. A long black scarf shrouded her blond hair, crisscrossed her neck, and fell down her back. She had on dark glasses, the same midnight-red lipstick, and drew more stares than the elephants and lions on either side of her. In spite of herself, Marie thought of Nora and Maud as entangled particles with identical polarizations.

"Sorry I'm late," Maud said, taking off her sunglasses. Her eyes were dry, hard, not a trace of tears, but Marie hadn't expected sobbing. "Your colleagues have become like flies on carrion," she went on. "I had to change rooms and reregister under a false name. I will probably have to change hotels. When I left just now, four reporters were waiting outside for me and I had to sneak out a back entrance. The most persistent of them is this Brilliant fellow from the *Post*. He sent me three dozen white roses. Do you know him?"

She put her sunglasses back on, but before she did she gave Marie one of those penetrating stares accompanied by a half-smile. Marie reassured herself that there was no way in the universe that Maud Blake could know about her affair with Ned Brilliant. Much like the pickup line, the knowing look was an old trick; use it enough and sooner or later it's going to hit the mark. Marie let herself feel a frisson of pleasure over Ned banging at a door she had long ago entered. Still, she couldn't help being impressed by the white roses.

Ned had always told her that one of her greatest flaws as a tabloid journalist was her inability to use her sexuality to raise the arousal quotient of her pieces. Once, after sex, he'd given her a little lecture. "As a writer," he said, "you need to use whatever it is you've got. In your case, you need to get a handle on your scruples. And I don't mean just the typical ones. I mean those complicated, neurotic, strange, funky scruples that pop up all over the place and get in the way. Take me, for example. You're having an affair with me, which you deem wrong because I'm married, so out of guilt you pretend that I'm the love of your life, which I am not, making you feel additionally guilty and confused. Professionally, I am using you to write my articles, which you find both flattering and abhorrent, but you refuse to acknowledge using me back, thereby undermining your own career. You get in the way of yourself, Marie. I'm not saying change. I'm saying figure it out and use it."

At the time, Marie had thought that this was just Ned's clever male way of diminishing his responsibility in their affair. But as Marie and Maud walked into the Native American Hall, passing three-story totem poles carved with absurd faces neither human nor animal, she thought for the first time that maybe Ned had a point. She'd had an affair with a married man because *it was the best thing for her at the time*—not because she had tragically fallen in love with the wrong man. Because he was married, she was able to enjoy the relationship without having to worry obsessively about the future—as she was wont to do—and could focus on her new career. And the fact that he was a good and seasoned journalist whose ego thrived on his role as mentor-competitor to her was part of the bargain. That she wrote his articles was a kind of apprenticeship. As Ned himself, rather ironically, always said, "The only way a writer learns to write is by writing." Although Marie felt morally ambiguous about almost every choice she'd ever made, she realized that there was nothing whatsoever to be gained if she construed her choices as not her own.

Maud took Marie by the arm and said, "I've always been terrified of totem poles—too much psychospirituality on a very big stick. Let's go see the blue whale."

"I'm sorry about Nora," Marie said quietly.

"She's been dead to me for quite some time. It's not as though I'll miss her," Maud said, then continued talking as if the little aside about her newly dead sister had been uttered and unuttered in the same breath. "I was very keen on seeing the space show at the Hayden Planetarium but just my luck it's closed. I understand they're rebuilding it."

("It looks like I'm going to be spending the rest of my life a dead woman." Nora Mars, *Two Deaths*, 1966.)

It occurred to Marie that Michael might think of her as dead, that if she was hit by a truck tomorrow, he might say, "It's not as though I'll miss her." It reminded her of a conversation she'd had with Marco, not long ago, on a rainy Sunday afternoon at the library. She had been taking a break from her quantum paper, sitting next to Marco, who was reading one of his magazines. At a certain point, he looked up from *MMWR:*

Morbidity and Mortality Weekly Report, turned to Marie, and said, "Death. That's it, death. You went into the philosophy of science because of death."

Marie put down *Automotive News* and stared at him.

"I just didn't get it," he went on. "As a discipline it seems much too wishy-washy for you. I could grasp the science part—child of divorce needs to order things—but the philosophy part? You loathe that abstract muck."

"Yes," she answered, "and it's why I quit. But I didn't always hate it. I'm as prone as the next guy to grappling with the meaning of life."

Marco didn't appear to be listening to her. "But what made you go into it in the first place must have been something incomprehensible, like death. You were scared into it."

"No, I think it was love. I think I had a crush on my physics teacher, Mr. Waugh."

"Someone must have died," Marco said, still ignoring her. "Who died?"

"No one died, Marco," Marie said, turning back to her magazine. "Of all people," she added, "I wouldn't expect you—quantum psychologist par excellence—to have such a classical Newtonian view of cause and effect. If this, then that. Haven't I heard you wax lyrical about the multiplex nature of causality? Aren't you the one who declared, 'Nothing has a single cause'?"

"Or it was something less obvious, less direct," he mused, ignoring her questions. "I've got it. Who didn't die?"

Much to Marie's surprise, the answer was right there on her lips—Michael—although she didn't say anything right away.

Marco went back to reading *Morbidity and Mortality Weekly Report* and she continued to read, or pretend to read, *Automotive News,* until finally she put down the magazine and leaned her head back against the chair.

"We were riding, no hands on our bicycles," Marie began. "I was twelve and he was ten. We were heading down a steep curved stretch of road we called Kamikaze Hill. Michael would always chatter to me about whatever came into his head, looking at me while he spoke and not at the road. He probably wanted to make sure I could hear him. I always stared straight ahead, not only to hear him better but also because, unlike Michael, I had to see where I was going.

"In the moment before the accident, Michael said something I didn't understand, so I looked over at him in order to read his lips. When I looked back at the road, there was a truck headed straight for us. Michael and I were each at the center of a lane. I saw immediately that the truck driver had one of three choices: to hit me, to hit Michael, or to swerve off the road. There was no time to think, so I rammed my bicycle into Michael's and sent both of us flying into the ditch. Michael hit his head on a rock and was knocked unconscious. I scraped a knee and sprained a wrist. The truck driver stopped, got out of his cab, and came over to where we were lying. 'You fucking crazy kids. You could be dead,' he screamed. Then he saw Michael and cried, 'Jesus fucking Christ, he *is* dead.'

"For weeks afterwards Michael would go around chanting, 'I almost died, I almost died, Jesus fucking Christ, I almost died.' He would make me tell him the entire story over and over and if I left out any detail he would make me start again."

Marie looked over at Marco, who was still reading *MMWR*.

"After the accident I decided that death was the Supreme Law, and the prospect of our inevitable death tormented me. For months, years even, I resigned myself to the idea that life was basically evil, where everything was doomed to end in death, and that all the stuff between birth and death was simply a pathetic distraction from that fact. And then I took Mr. Waugh's physics class—the one I was in together with Michael—and distraction gained entirely new meaning.

"One day he announced to the class that he was going to tell us a story about Erwin Schrödinger's cat. The Austrian scientist, he told us, put his cat in a box with a phial of poison attached to a hammer mechanism. The hammer, if triggered, would fall and break the phial and kill the cat. A lump of radioactive material was placed nearby. The hammer would be triggered by an electron emitted when an atom from the lump decayed. He explained how there was no way to determine if and when the atom would decay for sure. There was only a way of determining the *probability* of when and if the atom would decay. The conclusion: all events on an atomic and subatomic level are purely random."

Marie glanced over at Marco. The *MMWR* was in his lap and all his attention was focused on her.

"By now he'd lost most of the class," she went on. "Kids were passing notes, whispering, drawing, or combing their hair, staring out the window, staring at the clock. But I was transported.

" 'But what was the fate of the poor old cat?' Mr. Waugh asked, standing up from his desk, his curly blond hair lit by rays of dusty sunlight streaming through the window—my angel of deliverance. He walked around his desk—he was wearing brown bell-bottomed corduroys and a patchwork vest—and sat down on the front of it. 'Is the cat dead or alive?' He paused as the class, with renewed interest, contemplated the question.

" 'Dead,' said Greta Gray.

" 'Alive,' said Joe Moon.

" 'This is sick,' said Tina Clark. 'I specifically did not take biology because I can't deal with dead animals. Can I be excused, Mr. Waugh?'

Veronica Sheehan asked, " 'Why doesn't Showdinger, or whatever his name is, just go and look in the box and see if the cat is dead or alive?' Veronica was the most beautiful girl in the entire school and a rumored airhead. She surprised everyone when she was accepted by MIT.

" 'Excellent, Veronica,' Mr. Waugh said. My envy was so great I quickly had to swallow hard and blink back tears, straining not to miss his words.

" 'The fundamental concept of the new physics, the physics you will not be required to learn in my class, says that until you have observed a system you cannot know what state it is in.'

" 'Hold on here,' said Fred Finkle. 'I thought we were talking about a dead cat.'

" 'We are,' said Mr. Waugh. 'Just as Veronica said, until we look to see if the cat is dead or alive, the cat is neither dead nor alive. The cat remains in some indeterminate state until someone looks in the box to see what has happened to the cat.'

" 'But the cat itself is either dead or alive,' my brother, Michael, pointed out. 'The uncertainty is in the mind of the observer. That doesn't change the state of the cat.'

" 'In quantum mechanics it most certainly does,' Mr. Waugh answered, beaming, as if Michael had just asked him the million-dollar question, for which he had the answer. 'The relationship between the mind of the observer and the state of the thing observed is indivisible.'

" 'I can't believe that Austrian guy killed the poor cat,' said Tina Clark with disgust.

" 'There was no actual cat,' Mr. Waugh tried to explain. 'This is what physicists call a thought experiment.'

" 'So it's a science-fiction story,' Joe Moon said.

" 'Are you a Scientologist?' Greta Gray asked Mr. Waugh.

" 'Will you marry me?' I wanted to ask but didn't. After school, I immediately began discussing the implications of Mr. Waugh's cat story with Michael. In nature, were there alternatives—at least on an atomic level—to being dead or alive? Michael and I debated this question, and hours of discussion led to the formulation of the First Grand (insoluble) Enigma: *Is death the end of being or only an unknown transformation?*

"The second enigma followed hard upon that one. If the unobserved cat—or particles such as quarks, leptons, muons, gluons, fermions, bosons, and neutrinos—existed virtually in various other superstates or superpositions, then mind and matter must exist in some form we are totally unfamiliar with. Hence the Second Grand (insoluble) Enigma: *Does mind depend on matter or matter on mind?* And what is their relationship?

"But most important, Mr. Waugh gave me a new way to think about death. Perhaps, it was more interesting than simply a definitive end. Perhaps like mind and matter, life and death were more intimately related, less of an either/or paradigm, than we could, as of yet, conceive. Of course, by the time I got to graduate school, I had long dismissed these ideas as immature garbage."

"I've got it," Marco suddenly declared.

"Got what? The real reason I went to graduate school and the real reason I left?" she asked.

"No, not at all. I've found the missing matter, the dark matter everybody's looking for. It's all those virtual particles you've been telling me about that seem to go in and out of existence at random, you know, like the cat. It's Bohr's ghost possibilities. The missing mass is universal potential."

"Possibly," Marie said. She took the *Morbidity and Mortality Weekly Report* from Marco's lap and began reading as he expounded on his theory.

At the time, Marie had felt a little foolish for having gone on for so long about Michael, Mr. Waugh, and death. But now, as she and Maud approached the Ocean Life Hall, Marie suddenly realized what it was that compulsively drove her to the library to continue working on her philosophy of science paper and why she would never finish it. *Her paper had become a replacement for Michael.* Maud had said, "It's not as though I'll miss her," but what she really meant was that she had missed her sister terribly every day for years and would keep on missing her whether she was dead or alive. One thing became very clear to Marie. If she was ever going to get her brother back, she was going to have to give up her quantum paper.

Maud and Marie entered the upper balcony of the vast two-story hall and stood silently for a moment in front of the ninety-four-foot replica of the great blue whale—largest of all animals living or extinct, the plaque said. "The beast has a certain awkward beauty, an unlikely elegance, don't you think?" Maud said finally. Marie nodded, feeling once again as if she were in the presence of Nora's ghost. In a flash, Marie knew what it was she needed to find out: what event or events had kept Maud and Nora so deeply connected—and tragically apart—for so many years. She thought of herself and Michael. She had to follow the trail of betrayal.

In the glass elevator that descended from the balcony to the ground floor and the Ocean Life Cafe, Maud turned to Marie and said, "As you go along, days, years, decades passing by, you believe it's all going to add up to something, and then you get to the end, and it doesn't."

Marie wasn't listening. Something about the sisters just wasn't making sense. Maud, the older one, was popular at school and starred in the school plays. The younger sister was a troublemaker, a rebel, a fish out of water. One acted, the other acted out. They hated each other, they loved each other. But they were, in some ways, parts of the same self. Nora and Maud, she remembered, had felt so interchangeable they had even switched names when Maud became pregnant and Nora went to drama school in her place.

"Of course," Marie said aloud. Maud and the waiter, who was taking their order, looked at her for an explanation. "Of course I'll have coffee," she said. Marie was once again amazed by that fantastic human ability to not see what is right before our eyes. And she was a tabloid journalist. She knew that it was the usual and the mundane—the things that were most intuitively apparent—that most scandalized people. Our history, our art, our daily papers, were full of stories about matricide, fratricide, infanticide, incest, infidelity. We all betray one another. That we destroy what we love, or, rather, what loves us, is comprehensible to everyone, and the truth of it is deeply shocking no matter how often we confront it.

("I don't play favorites. I have betrayed everyone I have ever known." Nora Mars, *The End of Sarah*, 1973.)

"You're not Rex's mother. Nora is," Marie said, a simple statement of fact. "She married her own son."

"Was. She's dead." Maud did not appear the least bit disconcerted. "Probably nothing more than ashes and a few bits of bone by now. I'm considering heading over to the piers later this afternoon and chucking her remains into the East River."

"It was Nora who got pregnant, not you," Marie explained, as if this were news to Maud. "Rex told me you and Nora fell out over a boyfriend—Rex's father was your boyfriend. Nora got pregnant with your boyfriend." Marie couldn't see Maud's eyes behind her dark glasses. Was this the right story? The wrong story? Just another story? Don't stop now, Marie told herself. "Nora had the baby and then wanted to get the hell out of small-town America. She was not the type to relish the role of Hester Prynne. How am I doing?"

Maud gave no sign either way.

"You told her to go to NYU in your place because you were dying to get rid of her. She had just about ruined your life when she slept with your boyfriend . . ."

"He meant nothing to me," Maud corrected. "Our mother died having Nora. Our father was ill and Nora's shenanigans were making him worse. I wasn't going to let my father die because of her too. If she hadn't left, I would have killed her."

("There's murder in every intelligent woman's heart." Nora Mars, *Two Deaths*, 1966.)

"Rex never knew about you and Nora changing names when Nora took your place at drama school, so that is why he believes *you* are his mother. The birth certificate his detective dug up for him names Maud Blake as his mother. When she gave birth, she was still Maud. She didn't become Nora until she went to New York."

Maud took off her glasses and looked at Marie through her sharp green eyes—the same eyes that helped make Nora famous—with such intensity Marie had to force herself to maintain eye contact. "Nora was a sick, misguided, and perverse human being. But I actually believe she was trying to help Rex by marrying him."

The same group of schoolchildren who had passed Marie while she was standing in front of the yak exhibit filed into the room. They stood in a semicircle near the door, silently staring up at the whale.

"Is that thing real?" a blond girl with braids asked.

"It's dead," said a boy wearing a baseball cap backward.

"And why are you telling me all this? After all these years of silence, why are you exposing yourself, your sister, and Rex to me?" Marie asked.

"I have no idea," Maud said. "Maybe it has something to do with you. Maybe it was something I heard in your voice, a look you have in your eyes, that made me want to tell this story."

"The funny thing about syrup is that even though it's sweet it's still hard to swallow," Marie said, wondering where that line had come from. Nora Mars was definitely nearby. "Why when I came to see you in Hopewell did you lie and tell me it was you who got pregnant instead of Nora?"

"Nora wasn't dead yet. I was trying to protect her. God knows why. I imagine these things are instinctual," Maud said. "But now she's dead and there's no use protecting the dead, is there?"

("Some people are better off dead." Nora Mars, *Sweet Revenge*, 1955.)

"What about Rex?"

Maud shrugged. "I believe it was Rex who pushed the first domino over. He led you to me, did he not? I cannot answer for his motivations."

Marie knew she had to dig a little deeper here, not for the *Star*—that story was complete—but for herself. Like quantum mechanics, or surrealist art, human motivations had some kind of absurd logic to them that was beyond our conscious comprehension. To comfort ourselves, we relied on obvious motivations such as money, jealousy, or lust to explain our behavior. But mostly, Marie believed, our actions are motivated by our efforts to distract ourselves from the deep truths, the paradoxes. Maud had twice pointed Marie in the direction of the sisters' mother. Nora Mars' scandal-ridden life, Marie imagined, was a distraction from her original scandal—*the murder of her mother in childbirth.* And Marie knew her quantum paper was, on some primal level, a distraction—not from her betrayal and loss of her brother *but from having caused her father to leave.*

"I've got a deadline to meet," Marie said, standing up, feeling unnerved by the influence Marco's quantum psychology was having on her thinking. "I hope we'll see each other again."

"Who knows?" Maud said, refusing Marie's money for the coffee.

When Marie left the American Museum of Natural History, a full-scale thunderstorm was in progress and she had no umbrella. Sirens screamed by as flashes of ghost-white light lit up a dark green sky—a summer storm in March. Thwacks and cracks of thunder made Marie envision ships crashing into icebergs, colossal bowling balls smashing down alleys, intergalactic war machines. She had less than two hours to give the copy over to Brewster. Luckily, the body of the story had long since been written; all that was left to do was add these last career-making tidbits. She didn't have time to wait, so she bolted out into the rain and became instantly soaked through as she ran for the subway. Flying down the stairs and out of the torrent, she wondered what headline Brewster would dream up for the story.

10

{LIFE}

*"If I had my life to live again, I'd make the
same mistakes, only sooner."*
—TALLULAH BANKHEAD

*"It is not true that life is one damn thing after another—
it's one damn thing over and over."*
—EDNA ST. VINCENT MILLAY

*"We used to think our future was in the stars.
Now we know it is in our genes."*
—JAMES WATSON

One week later Marie was sitting on a bench watching six giraffes and four ostriches, deliberating over why the zookeepers
at the Bronx Zoo had decided to put them in the same enclo-
sure. Was it an aesthetic choice because they both had long
necks, or was there a zoological purpose? The heat wave was

still in full force and the zoo, for March, was uncommonly crowded. On her way over to the giraffes Marie had counted sixteen families, five couples, four groups of foreign tourists, and two other loners like herself. A small white picket fence, a wire-mesh barrier, and a wide and deep ditch lay between Marie and the giraffes. Scrawled across the picket fence slats in red Magic Marker was a giraffe-inspired quip: *Your attitude determines your altitude*.

Professionally, Marie's attitude was somewhere near Pluto. Her cover story the previous Monday—entitled OEDIPUS REX—had been a huge success for the *Star*. The paper sold out entirely and on Tuesday every tabloid in the country had dug a photo of Nora and Rex from their archives and put it on the cover. By Thursday the *Star*'s circulation was up by 100,000. The nontabloids, including the *New York Times*, the *Washington Post*, and the *Wall Street Journal*, all mentioned Marie's article in follow-up pieces on Nora Mars' death.

In what Brewster deemed the true measure of her success, Marie was vilified in print, on the radio and television, in letters to the editor, personal letters, phone calls. Two of the worst headlines were GRAVEDIGGING *STAR* REPORTER UNEARTHS DIVA'S SECRETS and JOURNALIST DRAGS SKELETON OUT OF DYING STAR'S CLOSET. Even the *New York Times* had a piece in their Saturday Arts & Ideas section that used Marie's obituary as a jumping-off point for an essay by a renowned postmodernist entitled "Selling Out Your Mother: The Primacy of Storytelling in Journalism's New Code of Ethics."

("The more enemies you have the greater your success." Nora Mars, *Checkmate*, 1971.)

Marie hadn't had time to absorb all that was happening to her because Brewster had immediately assigned her a string of feature stories on various aspects of Nora Mars' transgression. She took an in-depth look at Nora Mars' childhood, her unwanted pregnancy, her sibling rivalry. She talked to psychologists who variously claimed that Nora was a borderline personality suffering from any number of emotional disorders including ADD (attention deficit disorder) and MPD (multiple personality disorder) and was herself most likely the victim of incest.

Marie led an all-out manhunt for Rex Mars' natural father, who, it turned out, had become a career officer in the marines. She profiled Rex's adoptive parents, Frank and Sheila Greene of Toulouse, Ohio. "Rex always did walk to the beat of a different drummer," commented Frank Greene. She did interviews with Nora's first husband, Joseph North, professor of Elizabethan drama at NYU (there had been no prenuptial agreement); Bruno Zimm-Mars, second husband and Italian film director (he added the hyphen post-divorce even though the prenuptial agreement forbade it); Olaf Mars, fourth husband and Danish movie star to whom Nora had remained married the longest—thirteen years—and who had publicly announced his homosexuality in 1985. ("Nora and I were viciously competitive," Olaf revealed. "If it weren't for her, I wouldn't be where I am today.") Troy Mars, Nora's last husband

and former accountant, was "unreachable" but Marie had managed to get word to him that she wanted an exclusive interview and he had agreed to call her sometime in the next couple of days.

At the moment, she was working on a roundup piece about other famous cases of mother-son incest, including Oedipus, Emmeline, the notorious story of the Los Angeles Hightowers, and the Sante and Kenneth Kimes case in New York City. (True to her word—and work—Marie did not reveal the fact that Rex and Nora had not technically committed incest.) And, of course, she would cover the reading of Nora Mars' will scheduled for tomorrow afternoon.

The articles had made Marie an instant celebrity in the world of tabloid journalism. Several scandal sheets from major cities around the country had already made her handsome job offers and two publishers had called about potential book deals. And yesterday evening Brewster had taken her out for lobster and steak at the Palm Restaurant. Circulation continued to climb, and, though all the other papers were now thoroughly covering the story, the *Star* had been there first. Over dinner Brewster congratulated Marie, promised her a raise, and assured her that if she kept up the good work she would only occasionally be asked to do a rewrite on an article not her own. Marie thanked him and said she'd think about it, noticing that his bow tie was askew.

"Think about it?" he asked, then drained his glass of wine. "What's there to think about?"

"I would like my own column." The way Marie figured it she had nothing to lose and everything to gain. She didn't want to leave the *Star*, and she had great affection for Brewster despite all his foibles, but if she had to, she would write for another paper.

After fifteen seconds of shocked silence Brewster said, "I don't know whether to laugh or cry. Your own column? One big story and you fancy yourself Nellie Bly?"

Marie had an irresistible urge to straighten his bow tie, and she did. Brewster blushed scarlet. "I want my own weekly column in which I write about subjects of my choice." Marie spoke slowly and clearly and confidently. "I want an increased number of features a year with my byline, written assurance that I will no longer be required to fact-check or rewrite, and a substantial hike in my salary."

"I'll have to think about it," Brewster said gruffly, although Marie thought she saw a mischievous smile hiding on his lips.

"What's there to think about?" Marie retorted and Brewster laughed. She couldn't help imagining that somewhere he was secretly proud of her.

Then he said, "Tomorrow's Sunday. Take the day off." Brewster never told anyone to take the day off and Marie wanted to know what exactly he meant by telling her to do so. Was he simply rewarding her for her hard work? Did she look tired? Was he concerned for her health? Or was this the first indication that he would soon be showing her the door?

Marie ordered calvados with her dessert. They stopped discussing work and Nora Mars and talked about the heat wave. Brewster told her how much he loved the weather, especially extreme weather, as it got people all excited and communicative. A particularly good break for the *Star*, he remembered, was when in the first few months of its existence there was a snowstorm in June.

"No one went to work, the city just about shut down, scientists and religious leaders made dire or reassuring pronouncements while basking in their fifteen minutes of fame, and everyone wanted to read any newspaper they could get their hands on. Sales skyrocketed." Marie knew Brewster was making a point with this story—*it's really the heat wave that's selling papers, not the Mars story; like the weather, stories blow in and blow out*—but she was too drunk to care. As Brewster put her into a cab, he winked what Marie perceived as the wink of a comrade, and said, "On second thought, you better come in for a bit in the afternoon tomorrow. There are still quite a few strings that need tying on the Mars story."

On the ride home, Marie tried to stop the alcohol spin whirring in her head by thinking about Rex. With all the hullabaloo, Rex and Maud had disappeared. None of the other papers carried quotes from them. Although Marie had tried very hard to reach Rex before the story came out, she hadn't, and as far as she knew he had first learned, along with the rest of the world, that he had married his own mother by reading Nora's obituary in the *Gotham City Star*. Since the appearance of the article, Marie had tried hundreds of times to reach him and had apologized to his machine at least a dozen times. She had even gone out to DUMBO twice, but he'd either gone away or was not answering the buzzer. She was sure Rex felt conned, betrayed, manipulated, used, sacrificed, lied to by her, for which Marie was genuinely sorry.

Marie then had what she could only describe as an epiphany (albeit drunken): outcome was ultimately beside the point; in the grand scheme of things it was the process of finding the outcome that mattered. She still had only a vague idea of what Brewster had meant when he said she didn't want it bad enough, but what she did want right then more than anything was to be back inside a story trying to find out what happened next. She rolled down the window as the taxi sped down Fifth Avenue past the Empire State Building, its top stories still bathed in shamrock-green light. Leaning far out and looking up, she yelled, "Life is motion." She marveled at the fact that she hadn't understood this obvious truth before. She was brilliant. She was drunk.

("Genius is the ability to see the obvious." Nora Mars, *The Diva*, 1977.)

The telephone was ringing when she walked in the door to her apartment, and found herself hoping it was Rex. She had long since understood that he was not the man for her (if he had been, would she have written the story?), but she wanted to see him again, if only to acknowledge that something, albeit convoluted and hurtful, had happened between them. On the other end of the line, however, Marie heard Ned Brilliant's cognac-smooth voice. The bottles of white and red Bordeaux that had accompanied her prime steak and three-pound lobster (she had taken the leftovers in a doggy bag) along with the calvados had combined into a heady aphrodisiac.

"Where are you?" she purred. "Why don't you come up and see me sometime, like now?"

"I'm in New Jersey."

"A mere bridge or tunnel away," she whined, considering the option of phone sex.

"You sound drunk," he said.

"Drunk with desire for you," she said, knowing she would seriously regret it. After breaking off their affair when he left for his new job at the *Post,* Ned had tried several times to rekindle it but she had successfully resisted him. There was a part of her, though, that was tempted to get back together with him just so she could have the satisfaction of leaving him. But all in all she was very fond of Ned and he had gotten her through some very tough years.

"What man in his right mind would get you drunk and then let you go home alone?" Ned asked.

"Brewster," she said, eliminating the seduction tone from her voice. Not on the phone, not tonight, not with Ned, she decided. "We were celebrating." She walked into the kitchen and put the doggy bag in her refrigerator.

"Ah. I see. Did you get a raise? A title change? Your own column, I hope?"

Marie didn't answer. She went into the bedroom.

"Well, anyway, it's why I called. I just wanted to tell you myself, Marie, your Mars pieces have been cream of the crop, top of the pile, freshly squeezed. I couldn't have done it better myself."

"I guess not," she said distractedly. "Where's Carla?"

There was a long pause before he answered her, as if he had forgotten momentarily that he had a wife. "Away on business," he said finally. "I just got the boys to bed. Anyway, I simply had no idea there was much left to scratch on that sniffer. Damn good work." He chuckled an intimate chuckle and, sounding like himself again, he said, "Of course, I taught you everything you know."

"So you tell me," Marie sighed. She began to undress.

"In fact, they say that the best teacher is the one whose pupil outdoes him," Ned said.

"That's what they say," she said, lying down on her bed with her shirt off. She had on her red bra, which she wore only on special occasions. The ceiling began alternating between spin and wave.

"When I talked to Rex Mars a couple weeks back," Ned said, "I thought to myself, nothing here but a casualty, a leftover, a lousy crooner waiting around for his liver to fail. I asked him a few dull questions to which I got a few dull answers, paid for half a bottle of whiskey, and left. I even thought fondly of you that day on account of the bar. Little did I know you were gonna scoop me."

"The bar?" Marie said, unbuttoning her trousers and trying to wriggle out of them while keeping the phone clenched between her ear and shoulder. The glories of multitasking, she thought.

"Now, don't get offended. I know how touchy—you might even say paranoid—you are about some things. It's a little place west of SoHo called the Ear Inn. I always thought it was so cute how you tried to hide that you're a bit deaf."

"You knew?" she said, sitting up.

"Sure. Everybody knows."

"Jesus," Marie said, quickly lying back down and very much regretting the second snifter of calvados. Both the ceiling and the walls now appeared fluid. She felt as if she were in an aquarium with the water on the outside of the glass.

"When?" she asked, closing her eyes in an effort to minimize the motion.

"Oh, I don't know. I believe I knew you had trouble hearing right away. I think it was the way you stared at my mouth. Hold on. I hear one of the boys."

"No, I meant when did you go to the Ear Inn with Rex Mars?" It took considerable effort to articulate those words, and until she heard Ned's response she was worried she might not have actually said them.

"I don't know. A week ago Thursday maybe. In the morning. I remember thinking it was a little early for Mars to be already drunk. Why?"

"No reason. Thanks, Ned. You go see about the boys."

As she fell asleep, she remembered the last time she had gotten drunk was with Rex Mars, and her sex drive had ultimately failed her there too. It certainly hadn't that fateful night with Simon. Tomorrow, she told herself, no matter what happened she was going to get in touch with Michael. She pictured him standing there in the car-rental place assigning her permanent bruised-apple status in his life. She was going to have to put up a fight. And then suddenly, she remembered that she'd left the package containing the oddly shaped blue bottles she'd bought from the Russian woman on the front seat of the Impala. She made a mental note to call the bubble-gum-popping clerk in the morning.

But by the next morning she'd totally forgotten about the blue bottles. She'd taken Brewster at his word and didn't go into work (she also didn't want to appear too available in the middle of a negotiation). She was at a loss as to what to do or where to go. It was the first time she'd had a free moment from her work at the *Star* since coming to her grand decision to stop working on her quantum paper and to pursue Michael. She wanted to call him immediately but she would have to wait until noon because of the time difference. She thought of the poster with the giraffes she'd seen in the subway on her way to meet Maud at the Natural History Museum: GET A NEW PERSPECTIVE AT THE BRONX ZOO.

As she sat watching the amazingly tall animals waver between treetops, she pieced together her conversation of the night before with Ned and realized that a mystery, even if minor, had been solved. She now knew why Rex Mars had been at the Ear Inn before she was. He'd been meeting with Ned Brilliant and probably a whole lineup of other journalists first. He'd undoubtedly made a day of it, scheduled one after another to come to his makeshift office fully equipped with bar. But why? Free liquor? Prepublication promotion for his autobiography?

Two of the smaller ostriches were running through the legs of the giraffes. She wondered if the giraffes liked to have these birds using them as a jungle gym. What if, Marie thought, letting her paranoid imagination run wild, that day at the Ear Inn Rex had been canvassing journalists to see which one was sucker enough to become a player in his elaborate fabrication designed to establish himself as Nora Mars' son and direct heir to her rather significant fortune? Of course, the question of whether or not Rex was Nora's son could be easily solved with DNA testing—and Rex had to be aware of that fact. Bodies were being exhumed regularly to establish paternity, descendants, identity. Yves Montand, Jesse James, John Wilkes Booth, to name a few of the most famous. Of course, Marie thought, you needed a body, or at least a part of the body—a tooth, a hair—and she remembered Maud mentioning her plan to throw the cremated Nora Mars into the East River. Marie panicked. What if some other paper got wind of this before she had a chance to suggest it herself? A giraffe stretched out its back leg and lightly kicked one of the strutting ostriches a few feet. Marie laughed at herself. Stories were like stars: they didn't belong to anyone, there were too many to count, and they just kept recycling themselves. With a mingled sense of sadness and excitement, she knew it was time for her to move on from the Nora Mars story.

A giraffe gnawed the bark off the trunk of a large oak. Another nibbled at new buds on its branches. In a Darwinian world, she thought, the reason for their height was obvious and beautiful. Their survival and their aesthetic depended on being able to find nourishment where others could not. Their irregular squarish spots helped them to blend in with the trees so they wouldn't be bothered by predators while eating. Biological life was so explicable, so purposeful, so organized. She had always loved Schrödinger's theory that life was negative entropy—that it began as a meaningless mess but was in the continuous process of becoming more and more ordered. The random, paradoxical, fluctuating, and uncertain nature of today's physics simply had nothing in common with the incredibly stable genetic information that governs living organisms.

The ostriches were prancing around the base of the oak like adolescent ballerinas in black tutus. Marie had no idea why ostriches had such long necks but she was sure there was a very good reason. The universe might remain an impenetrable mystery, Marie thought, but, with the human genome project deciphering all 3 billion letters of human DNA, the human organism would soon be fully understood.

Marie remembered Marco's insistence the other day in the library that the universe was actually an enormously large-scale version of life itself. His definitive proof was an illustration in the *New York Times* of a supercluster of galaxies put together from X-ray satellites and new telescopes.

"What do you see?" he asked her excitedly, holding the illustration close to her face.

"A strip of orange, blue, and pink disks of varying sizes," she answered.

" 'Galaxy clusters,' " he read to her from the article, " 'appear to be linked in web-like structures that stretch across space in long and thin strands. A supercluster often consists of two long intertwining filaments of connecting galaxy clusters.' Now look again," he said, pressing the newspaper in front of her nose. "What do you see?"

Marie shrugged. "A strip of orange, blue, and pink disks of varying sizes," she repeated.

"It's a cosmic double helix," he said with absolute certainty. "It's a universe-size coiled double ribbon of DNA."

Marie stared at the picture for a while. "I guess I can see it," she said.

"And even more amazing, the cosmic chemistry of deep space—a lot of water and organic chemicals—matches that of the human body much better than the earth's general makeup does."

"So," Marie said, picking up a copy of *Saveur*, "what you're saying is that we are really just tiny organisms living in a much, much larger organism."

Marco nodded in the affirmative, his dark eyes glistening. "And did you know that certain amoebas, when their survival is threatened, join together to form an organism that rotates and forms a flat spiral shape with a hole at its center?"

"Don't tell me, let me guess. I bet that under a microscope the organism looks uncannily like a spiral galaxy?"

Marco appeared awestruck. "How did you know?"

"Once again," Marie said, shaking her head, "you are confusing reality with a *Twilight Zone* episode."

"Science fiction predicted black holes long before they were even dreamed of by physicists," Marco stated.

"Actually," Marie said, putting down *Saveur* and leaning back in her chair, "according to Robert Nozick's principle of fecundity, you are right."

"Principle of fecundity?"

As Marie expected, Marco perked right up.

"It states that all possibilities are realized, while it itself is one of those possibilities."

Marco leaned close to Marie. He smelled of cucumbers. "Did you know," he said in a whisper, "that nearly 97 percent of DNA—known as junk DNA—has no coding purposes? Its function is still unknown."

"Yes," Marie whispered back, wondering why she was whispering. "They suspect it contains obsolete information that was once necessary in the early stages of our evolution."

"But did you also realize"—he could barely contain his glee—"that around 97 percent of the universe is made up of dark matter, that mass or energy no one seems able to find? Don't you think those two percentages a phenomenal coincidence?"

"Did you know," Marie said, "that the number of heartbeats during the average stay on earth is roughly the same for all animals—around 1 billion?"

Marco would not be distracted from his argument. He read again from the *Times*. " 'Superclusters are typically seen as being comprised of clusters and galaxies, intracluster gases and, presumably, dark matter, the invisible stuff that constitutes most of the universe's mass and gravitational force.' "

"I'm sorry, but I don't get it," Marie said, now riffling through *Car and Driver*.

He sighed. "The point is that dark matter and junk DNA could be related somehow. Dark matter may be the cosmic equivalent of junk DNA. Solve the problem of dark matter and you'll discover the meaning of junk DNA and vice versa."

Marie put down the magazine, pulled out her cell phone, and started to make a call.

"You're not allowed to do that in here," Marco said. "Who are you calling?"

"Sweden," Marie said. "The Nobel committee ought to know about this."

"Do you really know someone there?" Marco asked.

Marie put her phone away. "It was a joke. Frankly, the only connection I see between junk DNA and dark matter is that quantum mechanics has made it possible for us to know that we don't know anything about either of those things." Marie supposed the genome project would eventually make it possible for her to know if spinsterhood was encoded in her DNA. She decided she wasn't going to wait to find out. "Marco," Marie said urgently, "I want to get married."

He looked up from his paper. "I know."

"Would you marry me?" she asked. "I mean like a white marriage, no strings, just as a kind of experiment to see whether it is possible to alter your own fate." Marie paused.

Marco was staring at her, expressionless. Appalled, Marie realized that he might misinterpret her marriage proposal as somehow offensive. "Of course, I don't know if you already are married, and I realize it's a big thing to ask of someone you hardly even know, and I'm sure it's just a terrible idea."

"It would be redundant," Marco said simply. "We already are married."

Marie laughed nervously. Why, she berated herself, didn't she think before she spoke? "You mean in some parallel universe?"

"No," he said, "I mean in this one. For better or for worse, we are, as I have told you before, inextricably, intimately connected. I consider us to be an example of Bell's theorem, evidence of interaction, further proof of the Aspect Experiment. We are two particles that, having come into contact, will continue to influence each other no matter how far apart we may move. As such, we are a force, a dynamic, an interaction. We are now part of a single system and respond together to further interactions. So, you see, we already are married."

"QUIP, you're describing QUIP, the quantum inseparability principle—but we aren't particles, we're people. In any case, Marco," Marie said, surprised she was offended, "you could have just said no."

"Did you know that the origins of life are still entirely unknown and that a leading theory is that life did not originate on earth but came from somewhere else in the universe?" Marco asked.

"The term for the theory is panspermia," Marie answered

snidely, not even attempting to follow his train of thought. "It was a ridiculous idea anyway. Marrying you to defy fate? I don't know what I was thinking. I just wanted to have it written down somewhere that someone once swore to spend his life with me." Marie slid down in her chair and rested her head back. "I did almost get married once, you know."

("Marriage can be far lonelier than being alone." Nora Mars, *The Affair*, 1963.)

Marco began to read the *Journal of Credibility Assessment and Witness Psychology*.

"He was from Australia, his name was Simon Sparks, and he was my brother Michael's lover. I was halfway through my first year of graduate school when Michael introduced him to me. I was immediately infatuated with him and began spending more and more time with him and Michael. I became obsessed with Simon—I read what he read, ate what he ate, came up with elaborate strategies for how to be alone with him. Finally, I realized I had to stop seeing them, which I did. After a while, Simon called to see what was wrong and we met at a little place called Marion's on the Bowery that specializes in martinis. We had several, and in a gin-soaked stupor I told him I was in love with him. He told me that for him it was love at first sight and couldn't imagine his life without me."

Marco was apparently enthralled by his journal.

"The following day Simon begged me to marry him and so we went to City Hall and registered to have the city clerk marry us the day after. Simon never showed up. I never saw him again, and Michael hasn't spoken to me since. Later I figured Simon probably just wanted a green card but couldn't go through with it." Marie closed her eyes and let herself feel, for the first time in a very long time, the full horror of what she had done to her brother. Sometimes life seemed for the most part to involve walking the line between how much hurting you inflict and how much hurting is inflicted upon you. Fall too far on either side of that line and tragedy occurs.

Marie decided there was nothing about giraffes that made any sense at all. They were so cartoonish with their silly spots, their wobbly legs, their ridiculously long necks, their Martian-like antennas, their jolly expressions. In fact, from an aesthetic point of view most of life was just plain absurd—rhinoceroses, hippopotamuses, zebras, mosquitoes, whales, yaks. Even their names lacked a certain grip on reality. Perhaps Marco had a point and biology and particle physics were just different ex-pressions of the same thing. She recalled Mr. Waugh telling her that if a thousand philosophers had worked for a thousand years *trying* to think up something of maximum strangeness they wouldn't have conceived of anything as strange as quan-tum mechanics. The exact same thing, Marie thought, could be said about life.

("Life isn't strange. People are." Nora Mars, *Edgeware Road*, 1966.)

It was getting close to noon and Marie hadn't come up with a strategy for how to talk to Michael. She figured she had avoided devising exactly what to say on purpose—it would be better for her to wing it. She reached for her cell phone in her backpack and, with a sense of doom, realized she had left it recharging in her kitchen. Accidentally on purpose? she wondered. She reminded herself that there was communication before cell phones and headed back toward the zoo's main buildings to find a pay phone. On her way back she passed a couple of orangutans tangling—playing, fighting, she couldn't tell which—on a ledge sticking out of a rock face. A mountain goat with large black spiraled horns stood above them watching. At a concession stand, Marie asked where she could find a pay phone and was directed to the reptile house. She wandered through the dimly lit building looking at huge snakes—cobras, rock snakes, bicolored pythons, boa constrictors—lounging behind glass walls. She watched as a white-gloved hand dropped a small rodent into a tank with a boa constrictor. Marie decided to forgo observing the food chain in action and moved on. A boy was talking on the pay phone.

"There's a big boa constrictor over there about to eat a gerbil. If you want to see it, you better hurry," Marie whispered to him.

"For real life?" he asked.

"Over there," she said, pointing.

The snakes—or rather the gerbil, with whom she was most identifying—had caused Marie's courage to dwindle, so she made a practice call to her answering machine. She had two messages. The first was from Troy Mars telling her to call him at one o'clock that afternoon. Marie looked at her watch. It was already a quarter past twelve. If she wanted to call him from the office where her phone recorder was, she'd have to hurry.

She nearly hung up but remembered there was another message. She thought it might be Troy again.

"Marie, I just got a package from High-Low Cars containing three blue bottles." It was Michael's voice. "Somehow I figured they were yours. I have, however, become enamored of their queer shapes and have decided to keep them under the assumption that they are a reconciliation present from you to me. And another thing. In your opinion, was our meeting in the car-rental place an accident in the cosmic immensity or the expression of some natural law prescribed in our collective DNA? I look forward to hearing your answer. By the way, do you know how hard it is day after day, week after week, year after year, to get a copy of the *Gotham City Star* out here?"

11

{QUALIA}

"I'm always running into people's unconscious."
— MARILYN MONROE

"God is in the details."
— LUDWIG MIES VAN DER ROHE

"I'm willing to believe that we are flotsam and jetsam."
— P. JAMES E. PEEBLES

Marie stood on the front stoop of the St. Cosmas Greek Orthodox Church on Eden Street. The World Trade Towers loomed above her like a state-of-the-art version of Jack's bean stalk. A rather large gathering of press—Marie recognized radio and television people from *Hot Copy, Good Morning America, Dateline,* and CNN and print people from *USA Today,* the *New York Law Journal, Weekly World News,* and *Inside View*—was waiting outside the offices of Burger, Klotz, Noland

& Windham, the lawyers for Nora Mars' estate. The reading of the will had been scheduled for Monday at three in the afternoon. Select members of the press had been invited to attend the reading (including Marie and Ned Brilliant, who was standing next to her on the stoop), but they had been asked to wait outside with the rest of the press until someone from the firm escorted them in.

"Here we are, sweating like pigs in March, and somehow global warming has become the nonissue of the century," Ned said, referring to the heat wave that was showing no signs of waning. "Not long ago people stopped using aerosol cans and had their groceries put in paper bags to save the ozone layer because they were terrified of burning up. Now we *are* burning up and no one gives a damn."

"Did a piece of yours on the subject get killed or something, Ned?" Marie asked.

Ned looked surprised. "As a matter of fact, it did."

"Try it again, only this time don't forefront the term 'ozone layer,' " Marie advised, thinking of all the ultraviolet rays she'd been absorbing on the church steps since her early arrival over an hour ago. "Instead, try using more third-millennium expressions such as 'electromagnetic theory' and 'gamma ray burst radiation beams.' "

"People are just a bunch of lemmings," Ned said, nonchalantly opening his notebook and jotting in it.

Marie didn't know how she had found attractive this know-it-all who was too skinny. She supposed she used to consider him intelligent and lean.

"Did you see Ray Bradbury's *Collected Short Stories* was on the *Times* best-seller list yesterday?" Ned asked.

"Yup, I did," Marie said, curious to know what Nora Mars had to say to them all from beyond the grave.

"I mean, you're getting as big as Oprah," Ned was saying. "You mention in an article some spurious story about Nora Mars choosing her last name from a Bradbury short story called 'Mars Is Heaven' and the next thing you know, the book is selling like champagne at New Year's."

"I am bigger than Oprah," Marie said, then added, "Taller anyway." She thought of Brewster and his snowstorm in June. "Look, Ned, you more than anyone should know that it's all a matter of, well, star alignment. From where we are, my stars seem pretty well aligned at the moment but next week something will shift and my stars will all be mumbo jumbo again."

"Stars, Mars? Is your next piece from the astrological angle?" Ned asked seriously. Then, seeing Linda Peachtree from the *Post* alight from a taxi, he made a swift beeline to her side. Marie speculated as to how long that had been going on. Given Ned's eagerness, her estimate was in days rather than weeks. She then considered why she still cared. Was it just a fact of nature that once you've slept with someone you will always feel a measure—even if it was as small as a Planck length—of jealousy for your replacement?

When Rex got out of a taxi in front of St. Cosmas just after three o'clock, his eyes met and locked with Marie's. As she stood among the pack of hungry journalists screaming questions at him in hopes of chewing off their little morsel of flesh, she felt like a cannibal being observed by her last meal. She turned away feeling guilty and ashamed. But then she thought, Isn't cannibalism largely a myth? There was no question that this was an eat-or-get-eaten universe, but the great thing about humans was that there was room for bargaining. Whatever had happened between her and Rex, she felt that some sort of agreement had been struck. She looked back at Rex, who, wearing his blue cowboy boots with an Armani suit, was striding into the law offices flanked by Ned Brilliant and Linda Peachtree and followed by a swarm of reporters. Troy Mars and Maud Blake both alighted from taxis soon after and made their way through the crowd. From where Marie was standing, it appeared that she was far from the center of things. She knew, however, that it was a matter of perspective. As she had discussed with Brewster the previous afternoon, the center of things for Marie was already somewhere else.

After leaving the zoo, she had gone straight to the office, where she found Miles Brewster sitting at her desk reading through some of the correspondence she had received because of her Nora Mars articles, including job offers from other papers. Marie had placed these conspicuously at the top of the pile.

"Pen-pushers are a dime a dozen," Brewster said without looking up. His bow tie was bright yellow with pink polka dots. "And what tabloid has any use for traits such as 'a fine wit' or 'a nifty turn of phrase'?" He quoted the letters. "In any case, one thing you're not, Marie, is subtle."

"And what tabloid has any use for subtlety?" she countered.

"You know, I did consider leaving those letters on *your* desk, but I figured they'd have a better chance of a viewing if I left them on my own." Marie opened her desk drawer and got out her phone recorder. "So are you going to give me what I asked for?"

Marie hooked the recorder up to the phone, picked up the receiver, and started dialing Troy Mars' number. She would really miss the *Star*, she thought, but it was probably better that she move on. Hadn't Ned told her repeatedly that you can't make a career by staying at the same paper your whole life? It was important to gain a wide experience by jumping from ship to ship. Besides, it was the only way to make a true salary leap.

"I'm pleased to tell you, Marie," Brewster said, crumpling the letters in his hands, "that your little ploy was entirely unnecessary. Your request for a salary raise, the title of senior staff writer, your own column, and an increased number of signed features has been granted. I'll be announcing the promotion at tomorrow's editorial meeting."

Marie put down the phone, unable to quite grasp what she was hearing.

"I'm proud of you, Marie," Brewster went on. "You've handled this story with real elegance. But above all, I am profoundly impressed with your hard work and dedication during the eleven years you've worked for the *Star*."

Marie smiled nervously, scanning Brewster's face for some telltale sign that this was a hoax. Or perhaps, she thought, her doctor had called Brewster and told him they'd just discovered that she had some terminal disease and would be dead in a week and asked if there wasn't some way he could make the blow a little lighter. "I do have one final request," she said tentatively.

"Oh, you do, do you?" Brewster said, standing up. "And what would that be? I gave you everything you asked for. But if you want me to beg, I will." He winked.

Marie smiled, acknowledging his use of her line uttered way back when she'd first asked to do the Nora Mars obituary. "That would be swell," she said, "but that wasn't what I was after, consciously anyway. I was thinking it's always best to get out while you're ahead, and right now I'm ahead."

"You could say that," Brewster responded.

"I'd like to take a couple of days to wrap it up, then get out."

"Get out?" Brewster looked worried.

"Yeah, find a new story, let the others play out the Mars thing. From here on in it's just going to be a feeding frenzy. As with any good story, it's become everybody's story, each writer giving it his or her own personal spin. It's the right moment— neither too early nor too late—for me to move on."

Brewster smiled and nodded agreement. Then he smoothed out her letters and placed them back on the top of the pile. As he walked off toward his office, he called over his shoulder, "Good thinking, Walter."

Marie was desperate to call Michael back, to tell him about what had just happened, then spend hours, days, weeks slowly working their way back over the last fifteen years. Troy Mars, however, was waiting for her call and she knew she should make it. If she wanted to leave this story with a bang and not a whimper, she knew she still needed to give it her all. But what if during her conversation with husband no. 5, Marie conjectured, an earthquake or an asteroid or a tidal wave hit L.A.? Or Michael simply had a heart attack, a stroke, or amnesia and was never able to speak to her again? A man with a southern accent answered her call and Marie identified herself.

"I just want to tell you," Troy said in a soft undulating voice, "how entertaining your articles have been. You've got quite a knack for storytelling."

"Thank you," Marie replied, wondering what it was he really wanted to tell her.

"I appreciate your poetic license and all," he went on, "but I just thought you might like to know a few factual facts"—he coughed—"as opposed to your fictional facts." He coughed again. "Don't get me wrong. I love to read the tabloids. They're far more gratifying than most novels. And I love how you have to wait a day to get the next installment on the story. The wait itself is almost the best part—so frustrating and titillating."

"Mr. Mars," Marie said gently, "I'm on tenterhooks. Please tell me about these factual facts."

"I'm afraid Rex Mars has pulled one over on you. He is most certainly not Nora's son."

The Nora Mars story was like an oil well that just kept gushing. "Tell me how you know," Marie replied.

"Nora swore to me she never had any children, and she never lied to me. I was her one true love," Troy Mars said with total conviction, as if this explanation absolutely settled the matter. "We never actually got divorced. We just told the papers we did so they would leave us alone," he added.

As Troy Mars rambled on about his and Nora's perfect love, Marie surveyed the newsroom. A group of interns and fact-checkers was standing by the coffee machine looking hungover. The obituaries editor, Edith Quick, was talking surreptitiously into her phone—the mole, Marie concluded.

Finally, Marie asked, "Why would Rex Mars want us to believe that he had married his mother?" Marie, of course, knew what Troy Mars' answer would be, since she'd thought of it herself during her own private conspiracy theorizing session at the zoo.

"Nora's worth quite a lot of money. As her son he might be entitled to some of it," Troy Mars speculated.

Money was like childhood, Marie thought. Sooner or later we all wind up back there looking for an explanation. If she had thought of it and Troy had thought of it, so had a lot of other people. Nevertheless, the same informed instinct that had told Marie that Nora had to be Rex's mother told Marie now that Rex was without question Nora's son. The doubts she had experienced in the zoo were the result of her highly developed paranoid mind. But because, in the end, money does rule all, she would raise the issue of the financial interests of Nora's ex-husbands in her pre-reading-of-the-will article for tomorrow's *Star*.

"Just as you, as her legal husband, might be entitled to a portion?" Marie asked Troy Mars. There was silence on the other end of the line. What a savvy woman Nora Mars was, Marie thought, always making sure she had what everyone else thought they wanted: first fame, then fortune. Of course, there was an obvious problem with this modus operandi: Did Nora Mars ever know what she herself wanted? Did it matter? Marie wondered. "What other factual facts have you got for me?" Marie asked.

"Well, if you really want to know the truth, Maud Blake is not Nora's sister."

"Mr. Mars, have you ever met Maud Blake?" Marie asked.

"No, as a matter of fact, I haven't."

"Maud and Nora could have been identical twins."

"Odder coincidences have been known to happen," Troy said defensively.

Marie thought of Michael, the Chevy Impala convertible, and the cloudy-blue bottles. "Anything else?" she asked, anxious to get off the phone so she could call Michael.

"Maud Blake and Rex Mars are lovers and have conspired to inherit all of Nora's money and divide it between them."

Marie thanked Troy Mars for sharing his "factual facts" with her and hung up. Instinct told her that Troy Mars had already spoken with most of the other papers around town. His speculations were sure to be tomorrow's headlines in the tabloids. She'd have to use the same information from a different angle—something along the lines of how money, like jealousy, has such a bad reputation yet feeds the imagination and inspires so much creativity. A roundup citing major works of literature and film that have used the plot device of the reading of a will would get the story going. She sighed a little regretfully, remembering her decision to get out while the going was good. For her the Nora Mars story would be *ending* with the will.

She called Michael.

"I've finally got it," Michael said as soon as he heard Marie's voice.

"You've solved the Four Grand Enigmas?" Marie asked.

Michael laughed. "No, I mean the end. I've got the end to your story, which, I might add, I have appropriated."

"Let's hear it," Marie said, elated. Michael was talking to her as he always had—jumping right into the middle of a conversation as if she had been listening in on his thoughts all along.

"It turns out that Rex is not Nora's son but Maud's son, however Maud is not Nora's sister."

"Have you been talking to Troy Mars?" Marie asked.

"Who?"

"Go on." Marie imagined patenting and marketing Marco's quantum theories of human interaction.

"Nora's father married Maud, who coincidentally happened to be almost the same age as, and look uncannily like, his daughter Nora, thirty years ago. Maud had a thirteen-year-old son whom she left to be brought up by friends in Ohio. Maud marries old Mr. Blake believing she'll share in his famous-movie-star daughter's wealth. But Nora's a skinflint and despises her father, and Maud never sees a dime. She knows of Nora's weakness for younger men, so when her son is old enough, she insinuates him into Nora's life and the actress unwittingly marries her much younger stepbrother. Then Maud and Rex proceed to grift some serious money off of Nora Mars." Michael paused. "How do you like it so far?"

"I'm riveted."

"Maud is greedy. And as the diva-turned-financial-wizard becomes richer and richer, Maud devises a way to get the whole pie. She and Rex get Nora's maid to feed her crushed poinsettia leaves, which put her into a coma. When Nora is on her deathbed, Maud poses as Nora's sister and uses a journalist to convince the world that her son, Rex, is actually Nora's son and sole heir."

"I like the poinsettia leaves. Do Maud and Rex pull it off?"

"Alas, no. The journalist figures out she's been an accessory to an evil deed and solves the crime."

"Wow. It sounds like the plot of a Nora Mars movie."

"Thanks. You know, your stories brought me out of a block. I've been script doctoring for years but I could never just finish a screenplay. I would sit down at the computer and stare at the screen and berate myself for not having used my math abilities to go into business. I mean, after all, writing a screenplay is so passé. At first the quest was to write the Great American Novel, then that was replaced by the Great American Screenplay, and now everyone wants to write the Great American Business Plan. I felt like I'd missed the boat."

"There's still time. Remember what John Wheeler said, 'Time is what prevents everything from happening at once.' "

"Ah, Marie, I always could count on you. In any case, I was pretty severely stuck until I saw your Nora Mars obituary, which I thought was so wonderful, and I got to thinking about you and how you tried graduate school and when it didn't work out you just let go of it and moved on to something else. I thought about how I've been holding my anger against you all these years, nurturing it, feeding on it, unable to give it up. So I sat down and told myself, Today I'm not going to worry about whether or not I'm Graham Greene, and after a few days I had written a treatment. My agent sent it around and a major studio is interested." He paused, then added, "And I've told them that Marie Brown of the *Gotham City Star* is my sister, which hasn't hurt things any."

Marie told Michael about her promotion, about Troy Mars' version, about her decision to move on to the next story, wrapping up after the reading of Nora Mars' will. She was about to tell Michael about Marco, but while she was trying to figure out how to explain him, Michael told Marie about his string theory.

"When we were in Niagara Falls and you went to the hospital because of your burst eardrum," he told her, "that night I lay in bed unable to sleep. I was alone because Dad and Patricia were with you. I saw a dark piece of string lying on my pillow. I picked it up only to discover that it was the leg of a spider with the rest of the big black hairy spider still attached. Terrified, I got out of bed and sat with my legs pulled up on a chair in the middle of the room until morning. I had all night to analyze my experience and I realized that it was not so much the spider that had scared me—it was that I had believed I was touching a piece of string. It was the ugly surprise of the string actually being a spider's leg that terrified me more than the spider itself. I didn't recall the incident with the string and the spider until years later when I found out about you and Simon."

"When I err," Marie quoted, "it's never on the side of the angels."

Without pause Michael said, "Nora Mars, *The Diva*, 1977."

After they hung up, Marie headed for the library. The day was still sultry and the library's air conditioners were on full blast. Marie spotted Marco immediately, wearing his navy-blue pajama suit and sitting in one of the caramel-colored faux-leather chairs in the reading room holding open the *Weekly World News*. The headline blared NOSTRADAMUS PREDICTS HOTTEST HEAT WAVE IN HISTORY: CATASTROPHIC SIZZLING IN MARCH IS A SIGN OF CHRIST'S SECOND COMING.

"Marco," Marie said, plopping down in the seat next to his, "I've decided to give up once and for all on my quantum paper."

Marco continued to read his newspaper. Marie wiped the sweat from her brow.

"Have you ever noticed," she went on, "how that phrase is really very positive—'to give up'? It indicates generosity and height, two good qualities. I'm just sorry it took me so long to realize I have been wanting to give up on that paper for quite a while."

Marco didn't look up from his newspaper.

"You see, I recently realized I kind of like being tall, single, and a tabloid journalist."

Marco pulled on his goatee, a gesture she hadn't seen him

do in a very long time, then put down the *Weekly World News* and picked up the *Financial Times*.

"And then Brewster, my boss, gave me my own column, in which I plan to write about science-related subjects, so the quantum paper just feels obsolete." Marie thought how normally she didn't mind Marco's lack of reaction to things she said, but this time it was just making her feel bad. "It means," she went on, "that I really won't have any reason to come to the library anymore, except maybe to do some research on an article, although in my line of work we try to keep research to the bare minimum."

"I've been meaning to ask you," Marco said, resting the *Financial Times* on his lap, "what exactly are 'qualia'?"

"Oh, Marco," Marie sighed, slumping down in her chair. She didn't understand why he wasn't responding to the fact that she might not see him again. Had she hurt his feelings somehow? Or did he simply not really care what she did? " 'Qualia' is a technical philosophical term," she explained, "for what a person subjectively adds to the scientifically measurable aspects of an object and is perhaps the basis of consciousness. So, for example, you and I both see that your suit is navy blue but you will never truly know the quality of my experience of that blue." The sky at midnight, pajamas and Yohji Yamamoto, happiness, Marie thought. "But, Marco," she said, sitting up, "what I'm trying to tell you is that I'm going to be a lot busier at the newspaper now and I doubt I'll have much time to come over here anymore."

Marco said nothing and Marie was disappointed. She had wanted him to object, to beg her to stay, or at least to make her promise that she would come see him once in a while.

"A theory of the Russian cosmologist Andrei Linde," Marie continued in order to fill the void, "is that consciousness is itself an intrinsic part of the universe—as fundamental as gravity or electromagnetism. He points out that our subjective experiences—our qualia—are the only thing each of us is really sure of, that all else is speculation. In fact, he says, our knowledge of the world begins not with matter, but with perceptions. So I know for sure that my blue exists, my sweet exists, and my pain exists. I do not need any proof of their existence, because these events are a part of me; everything else is a theory." Marie paused, wanting to add, And you, Marco, are like this for me, more real and more a part of me than anyone I have ever known. Stunned by the emergence of these unexpected feelings for Marco, Marie continued somewhat randomly, a little desperately.

"Linde says that in order to explain the source of these perceptions, we choose to posit the existence of an outside reality, which in turn makes it easier for us to survive. Most scientists, however, find the study of consciousness problematic. Science is supposed to be objective and consciousness is inherently subjective. Traditionally, the existence of a real world separate from us has been a fundamental belief of all serious practitioners of science. But what if we have reached a place in our evolution, as Linde suggests, in which we now choose to recognize consciousness as a force of nature because it is necessary to our survival that we do so?"

"Such a theory," Marco said, looking like the Cheshire cat, "places us squarely back at the center of things."

"Yes, and even the most conservative scientists are forced to acknowledge the possibility that something called the anthropic principle is at work in the universe and may be the key to formulating a theory of everything." Marie stared at Marco's hands. She wondered if he knew how beautiful they were.

"The anthropic principle?" Marco asked, although Marie suspected Marco probably already knew all about it.

"It states that the laws of nature should allow for the existence of intelligent beings who can ask about the laws of nature. In other words, it proposes that one way or another the universe has been specially tailored to enable the emergence of life. It's a way of accounting for the incredible cosmological coincidences that have made life possible. For example, if gravity were even minimally stronger or weaker, galaxies, solar systems, and stars could not have formed to produce the atoms that made the biological molecules. Or if the electromagnetic force were any weaker or stronger, stable atoms could not form because electrons would not persist in their orbitals. Our atmosphere is penetrated by just enough cosmic background radiation to induce mutations in biological organisms, which helps drive evolution. At the same time, our atmosphere acts as enough of a shield to keep too many of these extremely energetic particles from killing us. Depending on your particular qualia, these coincidences signify that there is a God and She does not play dice with the universe; or that life is a quirk in a universe of random events; or that all phenomena, including life, are in the mind."

"So which of these stories do you believe?" Marco asked.

"All of them, none of them," she answered.

("Everybody should believe in something; I believe I'll have another drink." Nora Mars, *Southside*, 1970.)

Marie remarked, "Einstein once said, 'I am a deeply religious nonbeliever.' " Marie was absorbing the fact that this was probably the last time she and Marco would ever see each other.

Marco said, "Sometimes I find myself thinking or saying something that sounds so much like you and I think to myself that's a Mariethought, that's Mariespeak. Has anything like that ever happened to you?"

Marie looked at him quizzically and shook her head no. She was too confused, too unprepared, to admit the truth.

He then stood up, gathered his papers and magazines, and, as he walked away, said, "You spin me like a top."

From the steps of St. Cosmas, Marie deliberated over what exactly Marco had meant. Did he mean she dazzled him or made him dizzy? Or was it simply his way of saying good-bye? In any case, she had decided she wouldn't be going back to the library either for her quantum paper or for Marco. That part of her life was over and she felt like Sisyphus relieved of his rock.

She watched as a youthful man looking like Perry Mason with grapefruit-size jowls and dark earnest eyes emerged from the building that housed Burger, Klotz, Noland & Windham. The journalists waiting for news of Nora Mars' will immediately gathered around him, sensing that he wasn't just a guy on his way to get a cup of coffee.

"It was Nora Mars' wish," he announced, "that the principal statement in her will be made public. Burger, Klotz, Noland & Windham kindly request that the pre-invited members of the press join us in our conference room on the thirty-third floor."

A handful of journalists rode the elevator in an eerie silence. Hearing from the dead was always rather disconcerting, but the general hope that Nora Mars would drop some sort of memento mori raised the tension. The conference room was standard—large oval table, upholstered chairs on wheels. A magenta and black silk-screen portrait of Nora Mars by Andy Warhol hung on one wall. A short fat man with eyebrows so bushy they looked like awnings introduced himself as Samuel Klotz, Nora Mars' longtime friend and lawyer. Perry Mason sat at the far end of the oval table shuffling through papers. Several other people, including Rex Mars, Maud Blake, and Troy Mars, sat around the table. Klotz cleared his throat.

"Nora Mars' last will and testament reads: 'I leave my entire estate to IAM: the Institute for the Abolition of Marriage.' "

The room was quiet. Maud put on her dark glasses and Marie thought she saw the hint of a smile. Rex took a swig from a silver flask. Marie was already hard at work composing in her head her final Nora Mars article:

From beyond the grave, Nora Mars reminded the world of what she stood for as an icon—Feminine Power. Husky-voiced, worldly, touchy, insolent, cynical, and sexually ag-

*gressive, her enormous popularity with female audiences was
largely due to her ability to unite apparently contradictory
visions of a woman's role. She represented both the glamour
of a movie star and the ordinary woman, who struggled to
survive in a world dominated by men. Her sacrifices and
disappointments never erased her sense of self or her streak
of selfishness. She would marry five times, deploring the in-
stitution of marriage.*

"That's it?" Ned Brilliant asked no one in particular.

"That's it." Klotz said. With a nod toward the young man
with the jowls, he continued, "My colleague will pass out
copies of the statement and literature about IAM." He left the
room. Marie followed him out.

12

{FATE}

"I used to be snow white, but then I drifted."

—MAE WEST

"Just remember, we're all in this alone."

—LILY TOMLIN

"I should have been a plumber."

—ALBERT EINSTEIN

It was the crack of dawn when Michael called—his crack of dawn, to be precise, since he was in California. For Marie, it was just before eight o'clock. He was suffering once again from what he called terminal procrastination, which had kept him up all night.

"It's me," he said a little breathlessly. "I've solved the Four Grand Enigmas."

"What do you mean solved?" Marie asked, rolling out of bed. "The enigmas are by definition insoluble."

"Baloney," Michael said. "There's an answer for everything. Listen, this time I believe I've really truly come up with a plot for my next screenplay."

"Baloney? How can you say that?" Marie began deliberating over what to wear to the library. For a moment she considered simply not changing out of her silk pajamas. She hadn't been to the Science, Industry and Business Library since she began writing her twice-weekly column entitled "Scandalous Science." Brewster was having a blast with the leaders. CHAMPAGNE AND VIBRATORS GIVE RISE TO UNIVERSAL CLIMAX was the headline for her last article about a grand unified theory combining chaotic inflation (the theory that the universe is just one of many universes that are appearing and disappearing like bubbles in a champagne glass) and superstring theory (which postulates that all matter and energy derive from tiny vibrating loops). The column so far was a success, and she was learning that the more wildly speculative her articles were the better her readers responded, which was not surprising since she did write for a tabloid.

"Easy," Michael declared. "Take the first enigma. *Is death the end of being or only an unknown transformation?* With the development of nanotechnology," Michael explained, "the distinction between living and nonliving, natural and artificial, brain and computer, will become increasingly blurred—much in the same way as fiction and nonfiction have become 'faction.' "

Grabbing her special-occasion red bra from the top drawer

of her dresser, Marie said, "You may have a point. I often think of my computer as a fifth limb. But go ahead, tell me what you *really* want to tell me: your screenplay plot." Marie wasn't *really* telling herself that the reason she was getting dressed up to go to the library was in case she ran into Marco, whom she hadn't seen since her last visit there months ago.

"It's a love-triangle story about a brother, a sister, and the brother's lover."

"Very funny. Besides, I believe I just saw that movie," Marie said, looking through her closet for her black jeans and her boots.

"All the more reason to use it," Michael said. "People love what's familiar. We're all just kids who like to hear the same story again and again."

("I have nothing new to say, I just have things I want to say over again." Nora Mars, *The Last Three Days*, 1964.)

"So what's the answer to enigma two?" she asked. *"Does mind depend on matter or matter on mind?"*

"More or less the same answer as for enigma 1: mind and matter are fully interdependent," Michael said matter-of-factly. "You see, the answers to all questions are found within the questions, and all questions are virtually the same question, so all answers are the same answer."

Michael obviously had far too much time on his hands. "And the third enigma?" she asked. *"Does the world obey a law, or is it only a chaos in which forces clash at random?"*

"Why don't you give it a go?"

"Sometimes, Michael, your pedantry is endearing. How

about," she ventured, "the world obeys a law in which chaotic forces clash at random?"

"Bravo. See how easy it is?" He paused and took an audible breath. "Okay, my real screenplay, entitled *Out of This World*, is for a sci-fi noir comedy set in the year 2998. There's this criminal couple, Bonnie and Clyde types, who are on a crime spree across spacetime stealing from zillionaires' illegal holdings: off-planet accounts, undeclared properties in severely redshifted galaxies, etc. Whenever the dynamic duo—let's call them Bon Bon and Dude—are about to get caught by the intergalactic militia, they manage to escape through a wormhole. Finally, the zillionaires get together and hire an assassin named Marlo Philips..."

"Raymond Chandler meets *That Girl*," Marie interjected as she made herself a cup of instant Maxwell House coffee.

"...to rid them of these annoying parasites."

("If Noah had been truly wise, he would have swatted those two flies." Nora Mars, *Dark Blue*, 1965.)

"Marlo Philips," Michael continued, "is in hot pursuit of Bon Bon and Dude across universes. One rule about multiverse travel is that there are no universes where you don't exist. So the characters inevitably wind up in one of their potential realities. So as they jump from point to point in the spacetime continuum the three characters must confront their various parallel realities and examine the choices they made in that particular universe. For example, in one universe maybe Dude and Bon Bon are married and living in suburbia with three kids, a dog, and a Volvo, and Marlo is their live-in nanny. In another, Bon Bon and Marlo are lovers and Dude is the sperm donor for their baby. Are you with me?" Michael asked.

"I'm with you," Marie answered, putting on red lipstick. "But has it occurred to you that you might be spending a bit too much time thinking about the future?" She wondered what Michael and Marco would make of each other if they ever happened to meet.

" 'My interest is in the future because I'm going to spend the rest of my life there,' " Michael said.

"Nora Mars, *Checkmate*, 1971," Marie answered. "Go on."

"An effect of passing through the seething quantum fluctuations causing wormholes," Michael continued, "is that for a certain period of time after entering a new universe you lose all memory of your other existences and gain it back at your own personal pace, if at all."

"A kind of cosmic amnesia," Marie commented, while looking in the mirror and noting with satisfaction that her lips and bra were color-coordinated. She put on a gray cashmere cardigan—it had been unusually cold lately—and left the top three buttons open.

"Precisely," Michael said, obviously pleased by Marie's input. "Marlo Philips has the quickest readjustment period. So, although Bon Bon and Dude have some lead time, she is gaining on them. And Dude has a very slow readjustment period, so Bon Bon has to figure out what to do next, while Dude continues to believe that his only reality is the one he's in—say, as Bon Bon's suburban husband with the hots for his nanny, Marlo Philips."

"It sounds interesting," Marie said, glancing at her watch. The library had been open three minutes already.

"Marie," Michael said, evidently annoyed. " 'Interesting' is what you say to your blind date when he tells you he sells pumps and valves for industrial machinery."

"What about the fourth enigma?" Marie asked, trying to hurry the conversation along. *"Is there a purpose to life or is it merely an accident?* Or is this a purposeful universe and humankind has a reason to be here?"

"Our purpose is to be here accidentally," Michael said with a tinge of brusqueness in his voice.

"How does it end?" Marie asked, giving in to the inevitable.

"I haven't figured it out yet," Michael said dejectedly. "I was hoping you might help me."

They talked for a while, trying out this and that ending, but all were either too predictable or too preposterous. Marie, growing increasingly anxious to be on her way to the library, finally convinced Michael that what they needed to do was mull it over for a few days.

Just before they hung up, Michael said, "You do know, Marie, that you aren't fooling me at all. I know you either have someone there in the apartment or are on your way to meet him and are desperately trying to get rid of me."

"That's entirely untrue," Marie responded. "I'm just going to the library to do a bit of research for my column." And Marie had convinced herself that this was the whole truth.

It was, however, part of the truth. For the end of the millennium, Brewster had asked Marie to do a series of features on what cosmologists were predicting would be the ultimate fate of the universe. He was very excited by the idea and wanted to accompany each article with an apocalyptic poem of his choosing. The first was to be Robert Frost's "Fire and Ice." For a couple weeks now, every time Brewster saw Marie, while winking and blinking those violet eyes, he would, as if words were bullets, shoot lines from the poem at her: *Some say the world will end in fire, Some say in ice.*

Marie had plans for pieces on the big crunch, comet collision, nearby supernovas and gamma ray bursters, false vacuums, tears in spacetime, and heat death through entropic profligacy. She was also putting together an article describing various survival options—or "stays of doom"—including interplanetary colonization, Freeman Dyson's incremental hibernation strategy, the harvesting of Hawking radiation from black holes as an energy source, the theory of the self-reproducing universe, and galactic rearrangement by means of asteroid manipulation. But the most outlandish mathematically viable proposal was for the creation of a cosmic Superbrain that could ride the infinite event horizon oscillations during universal gravitational collapse, allowing for the eternal simulations of imaginary worlds in what one physicist described as "an orgy of virtual reality." All of these plans would need several gazillion years to be implemented, unless, of course, the latter was already in effect.

"Truth is entirely a matter of style," Michael quoted.

"Nora Mars, *Evil Love*, 1962. I'll call you later." She hung up, grabbed her coat, and headed out the door.

It was a very chilly October morning, so Marie walked fast. The store windows along Thirty-fourth Street were full of pumpkins, skeletons, and witches, and for a while now the Empire State Building had been dressed up nightly in orange. But today it stood undisguised with its head mostly in the clouds.

Over the past several months, Marie had been doing everything in her power to make the fifteen years of silence between Michael and herself vanish. He called her several times a day to tell her about movie ideas and to ask her advice about the Nora Mars screenplay he had sold for a small fortune to an up-and-coming studio. He was in his sixth rewrite and complaining bitterly.

("Success is when you are finally able to enjoy complaining." Nora Mars, *The Diva*, 1977.)

They talked to each other with such ease, it was as if those years hadn't happened, as if they were the result of a time-dilation effect existing in some other reality's now. On the other hand, Marie knew it was a bad idea to let what had happened between them go entirely unacknowledged. She had tried to apologize further to Michael by writing one of her first columns on the scientific study of forgiveness. Various research projects in the fields of cooperative game theory, brain imaging, the onset of AIDS, and primatology had produced convincing evidence that when the mind is in a state of forgiveness the immune system is significantly bolstered. The findings had led at least one psychologist to hypothesize that the martyrdom integral to most religious systems was in fact an evolutionary necessity.

Secretly hoping that Marco might have begun reading the *Star*, she added the following paragraph to the end of the piece:

> *Forgiveness studies are part of the growing field of quantum psychology, a twenty-first-century approach to the human mind which resists pathologizing the concept that a person exists in more than one and perhaps several realities. Some practitioners even predict an infinity of realities, each varying by infinitesimal shifts in perspective. Presently, humans are unable to control in which reality they find themselves but many quantum psychologists believe that the human mind is on the evolutionary brink of having the capability to travel or "leap" at will among quantum psychological states.*

Brewster had queried her about this addendum and she responded that the information was on the up-and-up, as she knew someone who was an expert in the field. Having read the forgiveness article, Michael had called and left a message on her machine saying, "One of my next screenplays will surely feature a quantum psychologist. How do you come up with these wacky ideas?"

The soaring, elliptical lobby of the library was warm and welcoming. As she walked through the reading rooms looking for Marco—if he happened to be there, she wanted to say hello—she saw that in the months she had been away the ghost of B. Altman's had all but faded and the reference books, computers, and sundry population of researchers had most happily settled in.

Marie had ostensibly come to the library to read up on the latest findings in the highly competitive and expensive search for proton decay. She had to admit to herself, however, that until then the Internet had proved a sufficient source for the background material she used in her articles. But she was sure that an off-line search for material would turn up a different set of surprises.

As she strolled around the library, pretending to be casually looking for Marco, she realized she was terrible at endings. Although she'd said good-bye to Marco months ago and hadn't seen him since, he was still very much entwined in her thoughts. At first, she had tried to perceive him as something of a bad habit in need of breaking, but after a while she realized that the harder she tried to forget about him, the more she missed him—and, to be dead honest, as it dawned on her that she might not find him in the library, she conceded that she was missing him terribly.

Once, after a late night at the *Star* and a couple of whiskey sours with Edith Quick (during which she had confessed to her treachery—having passed along to Ned news of Marie's progress on the Mars story only to be dumped for Linda Peachtree when the story was on the wane), Marie had returned home to search her apartment for the card Marco had given her when they first met. She knew she hadn't thrown it away because every time she came across it she always told herself that she really ought to throw the card out. As she went through her apartment inch by inch—all too brief an undertaking, given the size of the space—she became more and more desperate to find the card. Drunk and dramatic, she panicked at the thought that Marco had never really existed but was someone she had made up. It would be just like her, she thought, as she stood on a chair in order to reach the top shelf of her bookcases, to have fallen for a figment of her own imagination. She didn't stop to analyze precisely what she meant by "fallen for" because in that moment she found Marco's card in use as a bookmark in the pages of *Finnegan's Wake*. Marie wasn't aware that she owned a copy of *Finnegan's Wake* and was almost positive she had never attempted to read it. Her only interest in the book was the fact that the term for the subelementary particle quark, the basic building block of matter, had been lifted from a line in the novel—"Three quarks for Muster Mark!"—by the physicist Murray Gell-Mann in the early 1960s.

As she read the card containing no useful information whatsoever—*Marco Trentadue, Freelance Intellectual, New York City. Spontaneous encounters only*—she was struck by a familiar highly charged wave of annoyance. Marie then berated herself for having been so worried about whether or not Marco was real. Even in her most demented and fantastical dreams, she could never have invented such a pretentious nerd of maximum strangeness and indeterminable charm. She had thrown the card in the trash once and for all, and had since convinced herself that if she just saw him one more time and said good-bye to him properly he would stop haunting her mind and heart.

("Don't look back. It'll get you nowhere. And if you don't believe me, just ask Lot's wife or Euridice." Nora Mars, *The Last Three Days*, 1964.)

Unable to find him, Marie began in earnest to search the library's database for references to proton decay: the phenomenon by which the discovery of the death of just one proton would herald the eventual end of all matter in the universe. As she waited at the circulation desk for some obscure particle-physics and philosophy-of-physics journals, she remembered that the last time she saw Marco she was at the center of the Nora Mars story. The whole thing seemed so long ago, although it had all been brought back to her recently. In the past week, she had been subpoenaed to testify in two civil suits. Both Troy Mars and Rex Mars were suing Nora Mars' estate—Troy on the grounds that at the time of Nora's death he was still her legal husband, and Rex on the grounds that he was her unacknowledged biological son. His autobiography, *Mother Mars*, had been rushed into publication and had been on the best-seller list for many weeks. Marie had read an advance copy, skimming the early chapters at record speed in order to get to the end, where she expected to find herself, and did. Rex wrote:

I learned who my real mother was by reading the Gotham City Star. *This might appear to be a cruel twist of fate but in actual fact the journalist responsible for digging up this ugly truth was doing me a favor. I had always suspected—even secretly hoped—that Nora Mars was my mother but never made any attempt to find out, believing I was some sort of perverse monster. Having the truth blasted out into the world somehow made the whole thing more real and less horrible and therefore tolerable.*

Rex's words pleased Marie, and she felt a good deal of fondness for him but she had to wonder at herself for having been so obsessed with him that she constructed elaborate fantasies of their long life together. She remembered how she had tried to detect in his every word some secret signal or encoded message telling her they were meant for each other for all eternity. Marie reflected on what it was that had made her knowingly persist in these delusions. A distorted sense of reality, masochism, nostalgia, a yearning to return to her childhood? Or could it have been, she thought, for the sheer fun of it?

She sat down in a cubicle that had a direct view of the brown vinyl chairs where she and Marco used to sit and talk. They had been empty since she arrived at the library. In one of the journals, she read: "Proton decay would guarantee the final annihilation of all consciousness, purpose and meaning, including any record that such things ever existed. Estimates of how long this process might take range from 10^{45} years to 10^{210} years."

"There's time for everything," Marie remembered Maud Blake saying to her after announcing her plans to attend NYU's Tisch School of the Arts drama program. "Shakespeare, Eliot, Einstein, they said it, so why shouldn't I believe it?"

Maud had called Marie about a month after the reading of Nora's will. She had sold the house in Hopewell and moved to the Village. "Your column is riveting," she told Marie. "I have always found science either intimidating or boring but I am beginning to understand that it is our greatest epic." She'd even become a member of the Natural History Museum. ("Did you know," she later told Marie, "that the whale comes from the even-toed ungulate order of animal and is a direct cousin of the giraffe?") She asked if they could get together, and since then Maud and Marie had seen each other at least once a week.

Although Maud rarely talked about Rex, Marie understood that Maud and Rex had started to see each other now and again, and Maud would be testifying on Rex's behalf at the trial. She told Marie she wasn't interested in any more money—Nora had long ago set up a trust for her that would last her lifetime. But she indicated that Rex was cleaning up his act—he was in AA and planning a comeback—and he wanted to adopt several children. He thought he was entitled to his mother's money, and Maud agreed. She thought it both random and cruel that Nora had left all her money to some asinine idea.

For the umpteenth time, Marie glanced over at the brown vinyl chairs. This time she saw an intriguing man with dark wavy hair and wide-set eyes wearing an exquisitely tailored navy-blue suit and reading the *Sciences*. Her heart skipped a beat. His goatee was gone.

"Oh, Marie," Marco said, looking up from his magazine. "There you are."

"I've missed you," Marie said, falling into the chair beside the man whom she now perceived as having much more in common with the Great Attractor than with Peter Lorre.

She couldn't help noticing that Marco's complexion was slightly flushed, his limpid eyes were aglow, and his lips had curled up into an irrepressible smile. She wanted desperately to ask if he had shaved off the goatee for her, but she resisted. There would be time.

"I'm in the phone book," he said, then added, "I've been wanting to ask you something."

It had never even occurred to Marie—a tabloid journalist—to look in the phone book for Marco. When it comes to your own life, she thought, sometimes the simplest things are so hard to figure out. Marie smiled, picked up *Aviation Week*, and as she began turning the pages said, "Ask me anything, anything at all."

"What does the 'M' in M-theory stand for?"

"Mmmmmmm," Marie hummed happily. "Mother as in the mother of all theories, M as in matrix, magic, mystery. Take your pick. Literally, it stands for membrane. The world, according to M-theory, is not only made up of infinitesimally small strings vibrating in a realm of ten dimensions but also of equally small membranes which come in nine dimensions and are actually called p-branes."

"How small is small?" Marco asked, pushing his magazines aside and turning his whole body toward her.

"A p-brane is to an atom as a tree is to the universe."

"That is very small," he said reverentially.

"M-theory is by far the sexiest grand unifying theory of the moment. It's especially alluring because it supports a theory that the universe is holographic."

"Although I've been hearing it every day in my mind over

the past months I didn't realize until now how much I have missed the real Mariespeak," Marco said, slightly perplexed.

Marco's words were exactly what Marie wanted to hear. The best way she could think of responding was to give him more. "In such a universe the information about everything in a volume of space would be displayed on its surface."

"So," Marco said, moving to the edge of his chair, "that would mean we are not at the center of things but on the surface of things."

"You could think of it that way," Marie said, sitting forward herself. "No matter where we are, I suppose we will always be inventing crazy new ways to pin the unpinnable, measure the unmeasurable, center the uncenterable." She sighed. "Unless, of course, a proton is decaying somewhere in the universe as we speak, or, better yet, we're living in a false vacuum."

"False vacuum?" Marco asked.

"One theory for the ultimate fate of the universe is that we are living in a false vacuum bubble inside a much, much larger true vacuum bubble. If a tiny bubble of true vacuum were to penetrate our false vacuum the bubble would expand at a rate rapidly approaching the speed of light, engulfing a larger and larger region of the false vacuum and instantaneously converting it into true vacuum. This would happen in a matter of microseconds, causing abrupt annihilation of everything as the bubble interior implodes into a spacetime singularity. In short, instant crunch. One concern of physicists," she went on, "is that the incredibly powerful particle accelerators built to facilitate high-energy collisions of subatomic particles might create a tear in spacetime and *cause* the vacuum to decay."

"So our search for the fate of the universe would actually anticipate its fate." Marco was quiet for a time, then said, "It's a highly imaginative and sublime idea and reminds me of you, Marie: always anticipating."

Marie leaned back and thought she could happily sit in the library and talk to Marco for the next million trillion years. She thought about how many times she'd rambled on to him believing, ironically, that her words were falling on deaf ears. But she realized that it was she who hadn't been listening. After all this time, she knew absolutely nothing about Marco. And yet somehow she had known him all her life. Ever saying good-bye to him again, she decided, would be futile.

"Marco," she whispered, "theoretically, would you like to leave the library and take a walk with me?"

Marco nodded, then started to rise from his chair.

Marie knew just where she would take him—to stand under the gold-leaf constellations and lightbulb stars of Grand Central Station's entirely inaccurate night sky ceiling—and there in the true spirit of anticipation she would ask him to accompany her to the inauguration party for the Rose Center for Earth and Space at the Natural History Museum on the eve of the millennium. But when she stood up she suddenly felt extraordinarily tall, and though she knew more or less how tall Marco was (short), she suddenly became terrified that he was actually extraordinarily small.

"I have always thought you were terrifyingly tall, Marie, but you are really not that tall at all," he said, subtly positioning himself on her right side.

Miraculously, Marco's eyes were—give or take an inch—level with her lips. "And you, Marco, really aren't that small," she said.

As Marie and Marco walked up the spiral staircase and across the oval lobby to the door, shoulders, elbows, hands, hips, inadvertently collided. With each touch came an awkward flurry of apologies accompanied by deep blushes of mutual pleasure. Outside, a light snow was falling. On the library's threshold, Marco and Marie stared briefly into each other's eyes, then set off up Madison Avenue.

("I don't think I'm the center of the universe. I know I am." Nora Mars, *The Diva*, 1977.)

ACKNOWLEDGMENTS

Although I am passionate about science I am no scientist—in fact, the only way I passed my physics for nonmajors class in college was by writing an extra credit paper on the life of Marie Curie. The science in my novel comes mostly from articles in the the *New York Times* Science Times section (I live for Tuesdays), and from popular science books such as Brian Greene's *The Elegant Universe*, Steven Weinberg's *Dreams of a Final Theory*, John Gribben's *In Search of Schrödinger's Cat*, John Horgan's *The End of Science*, John D. Barrow and Frank J. Tipler's *The Anthropic Cosmological Principle*, and everything written by Paul Davies. I am deeply indebted to these wondrous writers.

As for the Nora Mars quotes, I have been collecting great one-liners for years from myriad sources including my grandmother, Thelma Stewart Brown, and old movies. I am also indebted to Autumn Stephens's wildly fabulous compilations. Great thanks goes to all the Divas who leant Nora Mars their wise words. Much appreciation goes to Tim Crouse who lead me to Roger Martin du Gard's "The Files from the Black Box," which I drew on often for inspiration and to whom I owe the succinct expression of the Grand (Insoluble) Enigmas.

For their loving attention to my manuscript at various stages I would like to thank Jin Auh, Sarah Chalfant, Grant Denn, Massimo Fedi, Ashbel Green, Chris Litman, Anne Maguire, Vesna Neskow, Lisa Springer, Grace Suh, Stephen Zimmer, and my enormous family. Very special thanks goes to Lauri Del Commune for her editorial wisdom and sage advice.

Above all, glorious tribute goes to my editor, Amy Scheibe, who is truly a genius with words and plot.

The Center of Things

Jenny McPhee

A Reader's Guide

A Conversation with Jenny McPhee

Amy Scheibe and Jenny McPhee first met while working as editors at Alfred A. Knopf. Their friendship grew over the years, and when Jenny wrote her first novel, she knew she wanted Amy as her editor. Their friendship survived the editorial process beautifully, and they sat down recently to discuss the finished book.

Amy Scheibe: What attributes do you think you share with Marie Brown?

Jenny McPhee: Well, I can tell you first what I most obviously don't share: I'm not tall, I don't have short dark hair, and I'm not partially deaf in one ear. I am exactly her age, but I am married and have two kids. I have four sisters, no brothers. Otherwise, a part of me identifies very strongly with Marie, with the overly analytic way she approaches the world, with her almost obsessive self-deprecation, and especially with her love of film from the '30s, '40s, and '50s. I am, of course, also fascinated by science, and in particular by the physics of the very small and the very large. That said, if I had to pick who I think I am essentially most like in the novel, it would be Marco Trentadue—a hopelessly romantic loner, a weirdo, and a shameless pseudo-intellectual.

AS: Nora Mars has the qualities of so many different movie stars rolled into one. Who did you have in mind specifically when you were creating her?

JM: For me Nora Mars is the uber-Diva precisely because she is all of my female idols rolled into one—there's a sprinkling of

Veronica Lake, a rather large dollop of Bette Davis, a dash of Gene Tierney, a peppering of Barbara Stanwyck, a hint of Marilyn Monroe, and many, many more, including my grandmother, Thelma Stewart Brown.

AS: In Dennis Overbye's review in the *New York Times Book Review*, he closes with the words, "Welcome to the trade, Marie." Did you feel like he was speaking directly to you? And if so, how did that make you feel?

JM:When I read that line at the end of Dennis Overbye's very generous review I admit I cried. In writing a novel and then actually publishing it, there is a lot to be very nervous about, but the thing I was most nervous about in *The Center of Things* was the writing about science. I am in no way a scientist. In high school, I got a C in Biology and a D in Chemistry. In the two science courses I took to fulfill a requirement in college I fared only slightly better. But it was in one of those courses—physics for non-majors—that I first gleaned that there was a deep and infinitely fascinating connection between science and art. On the first day of class, the physics professor, probably thirty years old with curly reddish-blond hair and shiny blue eyes, began the lesson by saying that at its heart physics was nothing more than metaphor. At the time I had only the vaguest idea of what he meant, but it sounded thrilling. The idea stayed with me and later, when I decided to write a novel, I thought, If I am going to do this thing that ultimately may not pan out, at least along the way I want to find out more about what that physics professor meant. So I took courses in quantum mechanics and cosmology at the Museum of Natural History, read numerous popular science books, and devoted my

Tuesdays to the Science Times section of the *New York Times* so that I could at least sound like I had some idea of what I was talking about when I had Marco and Marie drawing their whacky connections between physics and life during their meetings in the library. To have Dennis Overbye, editor of the *New York Times* Science Times, so graciously welcome Marie to the trade allowed me to heave a huge sigh of relief, but it also made me incredibly proud of Marie.

AS: Do you think science will always play a role in your fiction?

JM: I have no idea. But I do believe science and art are integral concepts, so on some level I suppose it will always play a role.

AS: What did you want to be when you were a kid?

JM: A writer. My mother still has stories I wrote when I was three. When, on my first day in college, a journalist for the student newspaper interviewed me about what it was like to be the daughter of a famous writer, I decided then and there that I wanted to be anything but a writer. I spent the next ten years rebelling against the very thought. But I continued to write all along; I just didn't tell anyone about it.

AS: Do you think having a father like John McPhee has influenced your writing in a positive way?

JM: Of course. He is an amazing writer, and just by virtue of being around him I hope to have picked up a thing or two. For sure, I picked up the desire to write—although my mother, also an excellent writer, was an equally strong influence. On the other hand, a Pulitzer Prize–winning *New Yorker* writer who is working on his twenty-sixth book is one tough act to follow. Impossible, really. One thing I very much love and find deeply comforting during the writing process, which can be at times agonizing, is the fact that I don't feel totally alone. Since two of my sisters are writers, it sometimes even feels like a family business.

AS: What authors have influenced your work the most?

JM: The writers I most revere are Shakespeare and Dostoyevsky. Apart from the sheer beauty and cleverness of Shakespeare's language, his crazy plots give me courage. That Dostoyevsky manages to put forth an intellectually scandalous idea on just about every page is deeply inspiring. Moving a little nearer to my place in the space-time continuum, however, Graham Greene's peculiar combination of humor, plot, and philosophy is something I aspire to. If I could create one character as intriguingly complicated as any of Dame Muriel Sparks's protagonists, I would be very happy. Ian McEwan and Margot Livesy are certainly models for me. In terms of theme, style, and structure, each novel they write just grows more fascinating and technically perfect. Of course, I could go on and on, but these came to mind first today. Off the top of my head, here's a list of writers I love to read: William Faulkner, Shirley Jackson, Carson McCullers, Flannery O'Connor, Dashiel Hammett, Jim Thompson, Raymond Chandler, Philip K. Dick, Antonio Tabucchi, Natalia Ginzburg, Thomas Bernhard . . .

AS: If you could meet one author (living or dead), who would it be and why?

JM: Dostoyevsky. I like to gamble and drink, and I understand he did both exquisitely.

AS: How did you set about researching the physics in *The Center of Things*?

JM: I read a lot of popular science books—a list is in the acknowledgments for my book. The articles on the latest advancements in physics in the *New York Times* Science Times were fundamental. I took several courses in things like the history of physics and cosmology at The New School, NYU, and The American Museum of Natural History. It was a process of absorption over time. I remember that, although I had been told a thousand times that space-time was curved, it meant nothing to me until one day Professor William Dorsey at the Natural History Museum repeated to me for the umpteenth time: "Mass tells space-time how to curve, and space-time tells mass how to move." And all of a sudden I got it. I understood. It was the most exhilarating feeling in the universe.

AS: As a writer, do you find it helps to write at the same time every day, or is that a myth?

JM: I don't know about the same time every day but that you write every day, yes. The consistency is enormously important for all sorts of reasons, but mostly because you don't have to overcome the ever-growing terror that comes with not having written for a while. I used to write in furious, periodic bursts, but I have come to learn that although there is something addictive about the stop/start method, you will produce a lot more and generally have a better time if you simply do it every day.

AS: How long did it take you to write *The Center of Things*, and how much of that was research as compared to writing the text?

JM: It took me two years to actually write, and I did the research as I went along. But again, I'm sure *The Center of Things* has been brewing in me for my whole life. To use an overused analogy, writing a book is something like having a child. You have no idea what you're going to get until it's born, but once it's born, it seems absolutely inevitable that it would be precisely that child.

AS: How long did it take you to get published?

JM: Not long. I worked in publishing for six or so years before I wrote my novel, so when the time came I knew what to do and, most importantly, with whom I wanted to work. So I am quite lucky that way. On the other hand, I have been writing since I was three years old, so you might say that it took me thirty-five years to get published. Oops. Did I just reveal my age?

AS: Do Marie and Marco live happily ever after?

JM: Of course. And, of course, it's open to interpretation. Is walking out together onto Madison Avenue in the year 1999, leaving behind their idyll of the library, paradise lost or paradise regained? I leave that to you, dear reader, to decide.

AS: Is Rex Mars really Nora Mars's son?

JM: I'm not telling.

Reading Group Questions and Topics for Discussion

1. What personality traits make Marie an unusual or distinctive protagonist? For example, Marco identifies her "chronic need to anticipate." In what ways does this quality manifest itself in the course of the novel? Do you consider it a strength, a flaw, or both? What other characteristics does Marie identify about herself, or do other characters observe in her (such as her passions for old movies and new science)? Do you personally identify with any aspects of her personality? Do you find her a likable heroine? Why or why not?

2. Marie says that her job writing for the tabloids is akin to assembling a jigsaw puzzle—a process that involves "taking a few facts, a little filler, and scrambling them around until they fit together into some sort of recognizable whole." In what ways does this process reflect the form of *The Center of Things*? What seemingly random pieces—bits of texts, storylines, genres, quotations, theories, and themes—does the author include? How do they come together to form a cohesive whole? As a specific example, discuss the use of the various quotations by Nora Mars scattered throughout the novel. What do they contribute to the overall narrative? Do they serve to illustrate specific ideas raised in the context of the plot, or do they act as ironic commentaries on the action?

3. Marie also says that the most challenging part of her job is "trying to understand people's motivations for what they did . . . because just when you thought you'd figured someone out, you'd see another possibility for what was driving that person." How

is the difficulty of assessing what motivates other people explored in the novel? How does the author show specific characters being motivated by a range of desires, ones that at times might even be considered contradictory? What mistakes in judgment does Marie make in figuring out people's motivations, including her own? How does this relate to the revelations she uncovers in her investigation of Nora Mars and her past?

4. Why does Marie worship Nora Mars? Consider the qualities that Marie admires in Nora in contrast to how she describes herself, particularly in her "litany of self-hatred." What does Marie's veneration of Nora say about the personalities we choose to idolize and the reasons we do so, and about the ways their example can influence us for better and for worse?

5. Discuss Marie's feelings toward Marco. How does she perceive him at the start of the novel, and how does that differ from her description of him at the end? At what point do you, as a reader, figure out that Marie is attracted to him, and that he is attracted to her? How does the author make this attraction clear to readers, even though it is not necessarily clear to Marie herself? What factors do you think prevent Marie from figuring out her feelings for Marco earlier on?

6. Discuss Marie's relationship with her brother, Michael. In what ways does it parallel the relationship—and conflict—between Nora Mars and Maud? In investigating the Mars sisters, what does Marie come to realize about her relationship with Michael? Why, if her relationship with Michael was so impor-

tant to her, did she risk destroying it by pursuing her interest in Michael's lover? You might also discuss the continuing influence her father has on Marie. Why does she say her struggle to finish her quantum paper is "on some primal level, a distraction—not from her betrayal and loss of her brother *but from having caused her father to leave*"?

7. Much of the novel consists of Marie and Marco's discussions about science, particularly about physics and quantum mechanics. What do these discussions generally contribute to the narrative? What is it like for you, as a reader, to encounter these ideas in the midst of a work of fiction? What does the author do to make these scientific theories accessible to readers who might not be familiar with them? Did you find any of the scientific principles discussed particularly interesting or intriguing?

8. Marie is particularly interested in making analogies between science and everyday life, and she and Marco frequently attempt to connect scientific theories they are discussing with specific events unfolding in their lives. For example, they discuss Bell's Theorem, which states that "any two particles once in contact will become 'entangled' and continue to influence each other, no matter how far apart they may subsequently move . . ." How does that description apply to characters in the novel and to their relationships to one another? Also, consider the idea that "a particle can have potential existences in many places at once until we look at it—only when it is measured by an observer does it become 'real' or fixed in one reality." What events in the novel illustrate the idea that "reality depends upon who is looking"?

9. Consider the novel's chapter titles: Time, Truth, Beauty, Jealousy, Money, Science, Love, Reality, Death, Life, Qualia, Fate. What do these headings have in common? How does each chapter investigate or reflect the particular theme or idea that provides it with its title? You also might consider the ordering of the chapters. What does it mean, for example, that Death precedes Life? Or that the novel begins with Time but gives the final word to Fate?

10. In discussing Einstein's theory of relativity, Marie says that "time, like language and meaning, was relative to its context." In what sense is time relative? How does this idea connect with the novel's investigation of such concepts as Beauty, Truth, Reality, and Death? Consider, for example, Marie's distinctions between "absolute truth," "tabloid truth," and "relative truth," and between "pure beauty based on an aesthetic hierarchy recognizable to all humans; and relational beauty . . . based on one's own perceptions." How does the novel illustrate the ways in which things commonly taken to have a single, objective meaning are actually open to varying, subjective points of view?

11. Marco's "theory of mutual good looks" states that "absent mitigating factors like money and power, people inevitably couple with their physical equals, their beauty equivalents . . ." Based on your own observations of couples you know or have seen, is Marco correct? Or do you agree with Marie, that there are *always* mitigating factors?

12. Midway through the novel, in a central chapter, Marie and Marco discuss scientific theories that place us "at the center of

things" versus those that place us at the periphery of the universe or claim that there is no center at all. Why do you think the author chooses to make this term the title of the novel? How does the issue of being "at the center" or "centered" relate to events in the novel, particularly to Marie's experiences and change of heart?

13. Nora Mars is famous for playing the femme fatale role in old noir movies. (If you want to check out classic examples of noir films, take a look at *The Maltese Falcon* or *Double Indemnity*.) Many of these noir films take the form of detective stories, in which the protagonist is somehow set up or undone by a femme fatale. These movies also often feature dark, tortured sexual relations, with stunning revelations, surprise twists, and multiple double-crosses. In what ways does *The Center of Things* borrow and play with conventions of noir films? Why? What other genres does the novel invoke? Is it, like Michael's screenplay, an example of a "sci-fi noir comedy"?

14. Marie, in attempting to account for what makes tabloid journalism and voyeurism such a "turn on," argues that "we look into other people's lives as a way of looking into our own," and we also "look into other people's lives in order to *avoid* looking into our own." Do you agree with her arguments? How are both of these motivations seen in Marie's investigation of Nora Mars? What do these say about why so many people are fascinated with celebrity gossip and scandal?

15. In science, there are two opposing views that Marie and Marco debate: one is that the universe is ruled by chaos and random

events; the other is that everything is predetermined by set physical laws. In philosophy, this debate might be seen as corresponding to a difference between coincidence and fate. How does the novel portray the difference between coincidence and fate? Which one seems to be the preeminent force that determines the direction of the characters' lives? Is it coincidence or fate, for example, that brings Marie and Michael back together—and leads Marie to Marco?

JENNY McPHEE is the coauthor with her sisters Martha and Laura of *Girls: Ordinary Girls and Their Extraordinary Pursuits.* She is the translator of Paolo Maurensig's *Canone Inverso* and cotranslator of *Crossing the Threshold of Hope* by Pope John Paul II. Her short stories have been published in many literary reviews, including *Glimmer Train, Zoetrope,* and *Brooklyn Review.* Her nonfiction has appeared in the *New York Times Magazine,* the *New York Times Book Review,* and *Bookforum.*